Play with Me
By
Fiona Myers

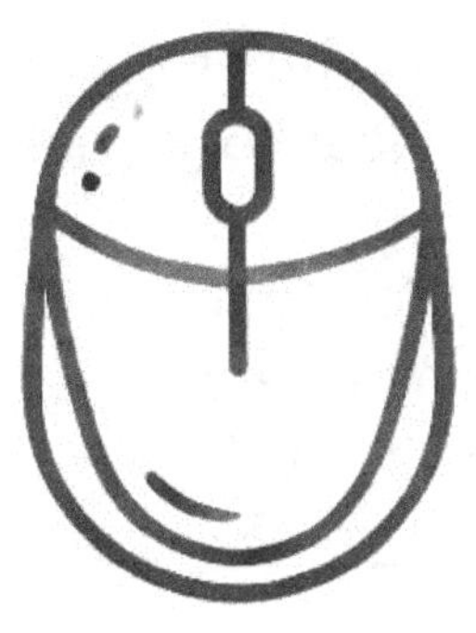

Books by Me

Into your being
Screams from the Barn
Feast of Shadows
From Ashes to Shadows
This isn't, real is it?

Listen with Me

Come little Children – Leigh West
Sweet Dreams (Are Made of these) – Marilyn Manson
Control – Halsey
Godless – BANKS
9-5 – Dolly Parton
Bury a friend – Billie Eilish
Gods and Monsters – Soap,Skin,Asfest
Playing God – Paramore
You Don't Own Me (feat G -Eazy) -SAYGRACE
Play with Fire (Feat. Yacht Money) – Sam Tinnez
Everything In It's Right Place – Radio Head
Dollhouse – Melanie Martinez
Why – Shawn Mendes
The Love You Want – Sleep Token
Mad World – Gary Julea
Welcome to the Internet – Bo Burnham

Scan me 

Contents

Dedication

To all the gamers out there who love to read and enjoy horror, this one's for you.

Content Warning

Please do not read this book if any of the below will trigger you in anyway.

Forced relationships.

Themes of manipulation, coercion, non-consensual control

Forced sexual relationships

Domestic abuse

Animal abuse

Mention of self-harm

Part One
Welcome to the System

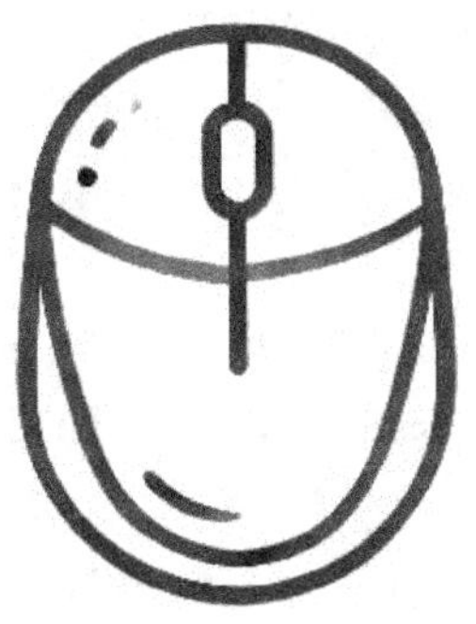

Chapter One
Press Start

I found this gem of a retro gaming shop thanks to a quick Google search. The shop is called Retrospective, but what Google did not tell me was that it would be in a dark, dingy back alley,

It is one of those establishments where you cannot tell if it's a genuine business or a front for something else. You know the ones you see on TV? A Laundrette, but in the back, they are cooking meth? That kind of vibe. Honestly, I am here for it.

I push the heavy door open, the smell of damp and sweat of the assistants working there, engulfed me. I held my breath to stop myself from gagging, the bell tings announcing my entrance. I take in my surroundings; My eyes scatter across the shop quickly taking everything in, I see arcade games like Pac-Man, Tetris, Space Invaders, on the left outer walls. All of them blaring obnoxiously loud. The excessive beep of Pac-Man making me grind my teeth. I close my eyes, take a deep breath, calming myself down, stopping myself from walking over to the machines and kicking the shit out of them.

I don't understand how anyone can enjoy that game; The repetitive beep beep beep, as it eats the stupid dots, the death sounds when the ghost catches you, none of it feels rewarding. There's no real sense of achievement. I force myself to zone out of the noise and take in the rest of the store. Desks line the opposite side of the shop; each one topped with a computer. Every single one is occupied by men.

In the middle of the store, is what I'm looking for, Video games; Endless shelves, stacked with titles for every console imaginable, in every genre you could think of. The lights flicker overhead as I walk through the aisles, waiting for that one game to catch my eye.

An unease starts to creep over me. I look around trying to figure out the cause. Then I see him. His eyes are on me. Watching me. He is sitting in the corner of the store, a shadow cast over him and he looks like a god-damn murderer. Glasses like BTK, beard like Peter Sutcliffe. (If you do not know who they are, Google it. They are not pretty sights.) He is wearing a chequered shirt covered in food stains. The way his almost-black eyes slowly scan my body from my shoes to my eyes, lingering far too long on my chest, Makes my skin crawl. His tongue pokes out, He licks his lips.

He makes me want to get out the store, but none of the games are jumping out at me. Frustration's building. I roll my shoulders back to try to release the tension. I breath in..and out... in and out... counting my breaths.

Just a little longer, I tell myself. Then I can leave this male invested place, I see the slight judgemental looks they give me as I pass them on the computers or down the aisle, then the not-so-subtle way they roam their eyes over me. If I was a man, would they be looking at me the same way? Absolutely not! I'm a woman though so of course they think they have the rights to me and my body. But they don't. No man does!

I move to the aisle on my right, careful to keep Murderer Lookalike out of my eyeline. Just knowing he is still there gives me the heebie-jeebies.

As my eyes scan the shelves, it hits.

A buzzing sensation rushes over me, followed by a loud, whirring noise in my ears, so intense, it feels like there is a balloon in my head expanding, my ears start to pop. I slap my hands over them, desperate to block it out. I want to scream. Beg someone for help. The pressure keeps building, like my skull's going to crack open, wax leaking out of my ears. I don't know what to do to make it stop!

I open my eyes, squinting, to see.

Then I see it a game. Poking out from the shelf in front of me.

My hand trembles as I reach for it. My fingers wrap around the dusty flimsy case. Then my fingers hit something sticky. I look at to see what I touched; it's a dark red sticky substance. I don't want to guess the many possible liquids it could be I smear it off on my jeans without thinking, along with the residue of it on my fingers. It still doesn't remove the grunge completely off the case though.

The sound disappears from my head.

I exhale, relieved.

I turn the game over to see what it is called.

SMASH.

Glass shatters. Pieces rain into my hair. Some hitting my shoulders. Others scatter at my feet.

I flinch, wrapping my arms over my head.

Then silence.

Total.

The Pac-Man machine stops. No sounds of people typing on their computer keyboards. No chatter. No music. Just a high-pitched ringing. I count to five before lowering my arms, slowly.

No one has moved. No one has even turned to look at me. The world snaps back. Sound floods the room. Pac-Man resumes. Conversation picks up.

Someone laughs in the corner. The man in the corner starts tapping his foot again, like nothing happened.

I look up. The light above me has popped. I am standing in darkness now. What the fuck?
A normal person would take that as a bad sign.
They would scream and bolt.
But me? I live for this.

Chapter Two
Payment in Darkness

I shake the glass out of my hair, turn around, looking for the cash register. I see it, I walk over to the desk, my legs feel numb from the shock of what just happened. A gangly teenager lounges in the chair behind the counter, feet propped up on the desk. Their hair's a greasy dark mess. I swear if you lit a match near them, the whole shop would go up in flames. Their face is saturated in acne. Squeezable spots, the kind where the moment you put that little bit of pressure on it, white goo would shoot out of it, because it's so full of gunk.

I wait, watching them. Imagining kicking the chair out from under them. Watching their face smash into the counter. Their nose breaking. Blood spraying. I blink. Once. Twice. Three times. Shaking the daydream out of my head. The teenager is finally holding out their hand. Waiting for me
to pass the game over. I smile and hand it to them. They try to scan it. The computer screams. **ERROR**.
Red, bold, flashing across the screen. Loud enough to make my heart jump.

They try again. Same result. Louder. They try typing in the barcode. Another error. Even louder. Sweat beads on my forehead. I don't know why, but I have the sickening feeling that they aren't going to let me have the game. The teenager sighs, clearly annoyed. Tries one last scan.

BOOM.

The computer explodes in smoke.

The lights go out. All of them.

Only the sunlight from outside lights the space now. Everyone in the store groans. There's frustrated muttering. Footsteps approach.

An angry staff member storms over to the counter

"What did you do?! The whole system has gone down again!"

The teenager extends out their arm to hand the game sheepishly to him, there hand has a slight tremble to it

"I tried to scan this."

I squint at the guy's name badge.

 Arthur – Happy to Help! Yeah, Arthur really looks like he is *"Happy"* to help. *Not.* I notice how the vein pops out his head as he verbally abuses

the cashier. It's not like they chose to make the
entire system break down, they didn't wake up
today thinking

 *"oh you know what, I think today I will break the
whole system"*.
That what annoys me with higher management
They blame the employee not the failing system.

Arthur takes the game, frowns, and walks over to
the Murderer Lookalike. They whisper heatedly,
glancing at me more than once.
Is he the owner. Why is he getting a say in this?
Goosebumps rise on my arm. Eventually, the
man nods frantically and pushes the game back
into Arthur's hands. Arthur returns, eyes on the
game, flipping it front to back. Like he is trying to
make sense of it.
*"So... We haven't seen this game before. We
aren't sure where it came from. Because of
that... we are just going to let you have it."*
He looks up at me.

*"We ask only one thing: that you do not bring it
back. No matter what happens."*

Chapter Three
Unstable Fantasies

This was the moment I should have turned and bolted. As fast as I could. Everything about this felt off. The red flags go round in my head; police sirens go off outside. Loud and menacing, telling me that all of this is wrong. There are two things I ask myself.

1. Why wasn't the game in their system?
2. Why couldn't I return it, no matter what?

Do I let these thoughts put me off? No, I do not!
I lock eyes with Arthur and slowly take the game from his trembling hands.

"Sounds good to me. Who could say no to an offer like that, eh?"

I flash a smile at both Arthur and the cashier. Arthur lets out a sigh of relief while the cashier just shrugs, looking as uninterested as ever. Before anyone could change their mind, I ran through the store and straight to the door. The

door slammed shut behind me. I didn't glance
back. I just kept running. I had used public
transport to the store. Thirty minutes travel. I felt
the game pulsing inside my hand as I placed it
inside my bag.
Weird.

I put my headphones in, to drown out the
sound. Time for my podcast - true crime,
obviously. This one was about how a bunch of
internet sleuths cracked a case before the police
did.

It's wild what people can do with enough data
and determination. Without the internet, I don't
know how everyone would function. It's odd to
think, how in the olden days everything was
communicated through paper and the News;
nowadays everything gets shared on every
social media platform, a child's missing?
Everyone in the community is sharing that post.
Body found? In the newspapers and plastered
everywhere. A fight in a random school? You bet
you are seeing that even if you are not in that
area. All of it instant, reported within hours, not
days.

Without it, I wouldn't have even found this shop.
I reached the bus stop and checked my phone.
15 minutes until the next bus.
With a sigh, I plopped down onto the cold metal
bench and waited.

Curiosity gets the better of me. I pull the game out of my bag, turning it over in my hands. I barely looked at it in the store. The cover was coated in grime, obscuring whatever was underneath. I wipe it this time with a tissue out of my back pocket. It doesn't even have a proper disc case; it is just a plastic sleeve. As I wipe the letters.

P L A Y   W I T H M E appears. Fifteen minutes flies by, I hear the *ssshttt* of the bus wheels as it turns the corner to the bus stop. I quickly push the game back in my bag and run onto the bus. I will find out when I get home what this game is all about.

Chapter Four
Mundane Tasks

The sun shines through my curtains as morning
arrives, birds chirping just outside my window. I
reach for my phone on the bedside table.
7:05AM. My alarm is set for 7:30 AM. I sigh,
once again, I have woken before my alarm. I
contemplate calling in sick to work. Just to
explore the game. It pisses me off how you get
home after a long day, and you barely have any
time to yourself. A few hours. That's it! Most of it
is spent trying to wind down from the bullshit. But
this game? It's calling to me. I know I can't really
call in sick. But the urge is there. I start scrolling
on my phone. A little red 1 shows up on
Facebook's Messenger. I groan. I already know
it's going to be some dumb shit. I don't usually
get messages from people; I like it that way.
I hate people.
They disgust me, the small talk, the fakeness. I
just can't be bothered with it all. All anyone has
ever done in my life, has let me down.
I open the app.

**"Hey Suse, Just, thought I'd drop a message.
I loved your outfit yesterday; it really**

compliments your curves. I remember how they felt underneath me, Do, you*?"*

URGH. Fucking Jeff. He works in the IT department at work. This man does not get the message. I give him death stares every day, actual *"if looks could kill"* energy and somehow, it only encourages him. He's so confident in himself it's nauseating. He genuinely thinks I should be flattered. That I'm secretly turned on by his creepy, unwashed energy. He makes my skin crawl. He's the blueprint of every generic IT guy but acts like he's the owner of the place. If he starts with me today, I swear to God.
I'll kick him in the nuts like he deserves or better yet, ram my pencil down his throat and watch him choke on it.
The vision appears clear in my mind:
His eyes bulged.
His hands clawing at his throat.
Thrashing.
Gurgling.
Until he finally drops, dead at my feet.
I get changed and head for the door of my apartment, something catches my eye as I pass my computer. For a split second, "Play with Me"

flashes across the screen in eerie green and red. I freeze.

When I look again, it is gone. Just my imagination; the game was in my dreams last night. Just the words Play with Me flashing on a computer screen repeatedly in big bold red letters, blood dripping from them, as if was calling me.
"Tonight, tonight, little game, we will have our time"

I whisper to the empty apartment.
For now, work calls. By the time I get there, Jeff is already loitering. I try to avoid making eye contact, sliding into my desk as quietly as possible. No luck. Even though he is chatting with Carol, my manager, the second I sit down, his beady little eyes lock onto me. I groan internally, turning on my computer and waiting for it to load. I try to make myself look busy, hoping it would give him the hint I'm not in the mood to be social today.
Nope.
Jeff practically bounces over, all smugness and misplaced confidence.

"Hey, Susie, did you get my message on Facebook?"

he asks, his voice dripping with fake innocence.

Looking around, checking to see if others are listening in. Everyone seems to watch when Jeff interacts with me. It's all just a show to him. It's like he wants people to laugh at me, or to listen in on some drama he is creating. He makes our interactions look like something more. My insides twist with discomfort waiting for the line he is about to drop. I think to myself, If I lie, it'll shut down the conversation he has already rehearsed in his head.

"Erm… no, I didn't. When did you send it?" My anxiety peeks, when I see the huge grin appear on his face, like he has just caught me in some big conspiracy.

"Oh, Susie. You silly thing, you. It tells me when someone reads a message, you know. It is rude to leave someone on read. Like it is rude to lead someone on, you know?"

I blink. Did this man seriously just say that? Does he really want me to call him out on what he did at the Christmas party? Is he delusional enough to think I led him on? That my screaming for him to get away meant I was asking for it? My blood simmers.

"Well, Jeff,"

I say levelling him with a look with a smile on my face.

"You'd think someone would get the hint when they don't get a reply. But I guess some people need simple things spelt out for them."
Jeff's face drops. That friendly, easy-going smile he puts on for everyone? Gone. In its place, the menacing look I remember all too well, the one from the night I rejected him.

A memory hits me like a punch to the gut. Last year in Carol's office. Me and Jeff, breaking into her private stash of vodka, laughing like idiots. I was already half-drunk, leaning against her desk, when suddenly, he was on top of me. At first, I laughed, thinking he was just too wasted and lost his balance.

"Oh, ha, Jeff. Funny. Get off me now."
I try to shift to push him off, I couldn't. My body's too sluggish, my drunken strength useless against his weight.

He does not move. Instead, his hands start wandering up my legs.

"Jeff, no, get off me!"
My voice comes out sharper now, panic creeping in. I shifted again; I jammed my knee between his legs.

Not trying to hurt him, just enough to create space between us, to make him realise I didn't want it.

"Oh, c'mon, Susie,"
he whispers, his breath was hot against my ear. He ground against my knee as he moaned

"I see the way you look at me. You know you want this."
His teeth brushed my earlobe, slow and deliberate. I felt his saliva hit against my earlobe.

My stomach lurched the smell of his alcoholic breath hit me like a smack in the face. Bile raised up my throat. I needed him off me, I felt trapped, my head was spinning, I did the first thing that popped into my head, I smacked him hard in the

28

balls with my knee, he crumpled to the floor.
I turned, looking for anywhere to throw up. I saw
Carol's half dead plant on her desk, not having
any choice, I grabbed it and placed it underneath
me.

"What the fuck Susie!"
I heard Jeff shout angrily at me, a bit of disbelief
in his tone.

I kept throwing up, the acid burning my throat.
My body kept heaving; my mind swam. I
remember thinking; How could my friend do this
to me? I never intentionally tried to lead him on;
we were simply good friends. Maybe everyone
was right, men and women can't be friends. I
kept thinking it was bullshit, ignoring everyone
who said it, but each time over and over, I get
proven wrong. It's exhausting. It makes me want
to scream.

When I finally straightened up, I wiped my
mouth with the back of my hand, I turn, only to
find him already back on his feet. He's smiled
dementedly. Not embarrassed. Not ashamed.
Smug. He stepped forward. I stepped back. My
heart slammed against my ribs. I swerved to
dodge him, but his hand snapped around my
wrist. His grip tightened as he yanked me toward
him.

"You dirty fucking slut," he hissed

"You fucking tease. If you tell anyone about this, I'll tell them you spread your legs for me and fucking enjoyed it, OKAY?"

His voice was venom. His entire demeanour had changed. Gone was the Jeff I once thought of as a good friend, this was someone else entirely. I ripped my wrist free and bolted. Straight to the toilets, in tears.

The friendship we had flashed through my head, trying to pinpoint all the things I had done wrong, what made him think there was something there. Was it the way I looked at him? The way I laughed at his jokes? I just wanted a friend, he understood me, so I thought. I didn't want anything mor

That was the night I knew: I could not trust Jeff ever again, our friendship was over. He never even apologised after. He honestly thought what he did was justified.

Chapter Five
Enter Name to Continue

The rest of the day went by in a blur. Going back into memories always disorientated me. Next minute I know, I was back at home in my dingy little flat. It's a bedsit sort of place. I can't afford much because my wage isn't high at all. The rent on places in this area is ridiculous as well. I don't despise the place. I just feel it would be nicer to have a place I can store things properly.

As you walk in, you are straight into my bedroom because I don't have a living room. The TV sits on a bedside drawer, on the left as you walk in. To the right, you have two doors, one for the bathroom (if you can call it that). There is a tiny shower and a toilet. There is no sink in there, to wash your hands you go to the kitchen, which is the door a few feet away as you walk out of the bathroom.

Basic kitchen really. Oven, fridge, sink, three counter tops and three cupboards. When you exit the kitchen, my bed is on the left side near the far wall, wardrobe in front of it. The little natural light is a window at the back of the bed, which means I don't have any choice but to wake up when the sun does, as it blares into my bedroom and on those winter nights, it's lovely feeling the draft go down my neck. The first few times it happened I thought the place was haunted, it felt like someone was breathing down my neck. Turns out there is a slight gap between the wall and the window. I have reported it my landlord, he doesn't give a shit. As long as I keep up with maintaining the damp out. I had to place My PC in between the doors of the kitchen and bathroom.

It barely fits in this tiny space, but without it, I would lose my shit. Games help me manage my anxiety caused by the bullshit of life. It is like reading, you get to immerse yourself in another world.

I've tried reading and listening to Audiobooks, but my thoughts are too loud to concentrate on the words in front of me or in my mind. The story ends up being a whisper at the back, like the little voice that always in my head.

A thrumming noise starts radiating out from my bag. I look at it curiously, then it hits me, the game is still in there! I open my bag, take the disc out of it. The name Play with Me stares at me reassuringly. On the front sleeve, it has a family standing together all happily.

"Build life, control it, destroy it"
it reads in bold black letters. I flip it over. It reads:

**"Play with me.
Ever wanted to play God?
Create life and choose what they do?
With Play with Me, you get to do just that.
With endless rights to create, you will be able
to do anything your heart desires. Just use
your imagination"**

Oh wow, this game sounds amazing. I have played a few roleplay games before, where you create a character and fight enemies. Usually monsters of some kind. I've never been able to create more than one character on those games though. I've heard of simulation games that allows you to though, but they've never really drawn me to them. I prefer action-packed games, see the blood spill out of the enemies while I slash or shoot them. Playing Barbie digitally never appealed to me.

The way Play with Me is worded though. To be God? All the ideas I could do in this game races through my head. All the destruction I could cause. I think this will be my new favourite game. I need a bit more control in my life.

The moment you are born, do you really have control? Your parents force you into this world and the government tells you how to live it. School, work, taxes, rent. They even watch what you eat or drink, what you are allowed to watch, wear. It makes me so damn angry. I did not choose this life.

The fact my dad made the choice to leave me too was a kick in the face. I did not have control if he stayed nor did I have a say in the matter either. I was always told it was a *"adult conversation."* He left when I was thirteen. Ran off with the local bartender. We always wondered why he was down the pub all the time. We thought he was an alcoholic, not sure which is worse to be honest. I was never asked who I wanted to live with. If I wanted to go with him? No. It was just, *"Susie, stay here with your mum."* It annoyed the hell out of me, like what kid would not have been fucked up by this?

I know my mum didn't have control over my dad leaving. She did, however, have control over how she treated me. All sweet, innocent, in front of people, then when we were alone, she would turn into the She-Devil. Telling me I am psychotic; I should go play on the motorway or even slit my wrists. I know I was in her space a lot when Dad left, I had no friends, everyone thought I was weird, so when your own mum

couldn't stand your company, it cut deeply.
Then she got worse when I told her about my
daydreams. Sorry Mom, sometimes I envision
causing pain to others when they've hurt me.
Seriously hurting them, to the point they can't
breathe. God forbid a girl has an imagination.
It could have all started when she smacked my
head off a wall because I smiled the wrong way.
Who knows?
But she always drummed into me

*"You can't act these scenarios out, Susie. You
will get in trouble, Susie; you will get sectioned in
the looney bin, Susie. No daughter of mine is
tarnishing my name"*

But in this game, I can, act all the scenarios my
brain comes up with. In some way, you know? I
rush over to my computer which would have
been top-notch back in 2006, jam the power
button, then the button to open the disc tray. I
put the disc inside and watch it close.
I turn the PC screen on. My usual files appear.
The Play with Me icon appears slowly. It has a
blood tear drop in the centre, The Play with text
at the top, then Me at the bottom.
     I double-click the icon and wait for the
installing box to pop up, I expect it to say it will
take hours, however, it's done within a flash.

Which is really good for this dinosaur of a computer.

The menu screen appears. On the left there is **Create Character** or **Exit Game.**

 In black bold writing with a white outline, each choice bullet pointed with what I am convinced is a droplet of blood. On the right, there is a massive house. It's Green, which reminds me of the vision through night goggles they use in shows like "*Help! My House in haunted*". The windows are darkened out. Occasionally you see a tiny light go across them, like someone is in there.

I select **Create Character.**

 With the bad day I had, I should create someone who has wronged me lately. Just to feel like I have control over them. I know, I won't have "real" control as it's just a game, just to make-believe, will reduce the daydreams from appearing so often. I can't work when the daydreams occur, they take over my full thoughts, actions. It's as if my body has been taken over by something else. Who has been pissing me off lately? Carol? George? Jeff? The postie? The President of the United States?

I know I am based in the United Kingdom, but it doesn't mean that his actions don't affect me. Most of the people's lives I am invested in on TikTok are from America, to see them scared, worried, makes me mad. I choose Jeff, the lucky thing. This may be the only time I choose him.

I'm reminded of how suffocating lately he is. How he is always in my space, and I can't cope with it. He makes me panic so damn much. His beady eyes scanning over me, that sly little smile. Yes, my minds made up, let's begin with Jeff.

Chapter Six
Digital Breach

This is it; I must get this right. It must be exactly like him. The idea of having my own little puppet of him to play with and manipulate, like my own very digital voodoo doll, excites me because the arrogant shit bag deserves it. Least this way its legal.

The text icon flashes. Daring me to go on. I start typing.

Name: Jeff

Gender: Male

Age: 32

Appearance: Brown hair. Blue eyes. Nerdy. Plaid t-shirt, dark blue chinos, trainers.

Occupation: IT Technician

I hit "**Enter.**" Pixel by pixel, the character begins to load. But… He does not look like Jeff. Too handsome. Too clean-cut. The character smiles and waves at me. Then I notice it, bottom left corner:

Not, right? Upload a picture

Huh. A picture? Do I even have one of Jeff? I think back, racking my brain for office parties,

Christmas nights out…Did we ever take a photo together?

Then it clicks.

Yes, we did. His first year. When I thought he was a decent before I knew he was narcissistic creep. I press the home button on my keyboard, search Facebook, and find the photo. I download it, saving it to my files.

My heart's starting to race. I return to the game. Click the **Upload button**. The computer makes a low whirring sound. As if it's thinking hard about what I have just done. The desk vibrates beneath my arms. The whole machine is buzzing now. Oh shit. What if I broke the damn game? Why is it taking so long? I watch the screen intently as, pixel by pixel, a person takes shape.

My stomach drops. It looks exactly like Jeff.

No, not just like him.

It is him. Every detail is eerily accurate. Except for one thing. Jeff is naked, his penis is limp, but his body damn hot. This man has a full on six pack! His arms are pumped. If he didn't have such a shit personality, I would find him slightly attractive. The game must have gotten his body from somewhere else; this can't be his body.

Do I… have to dress him?

He blinks rapidly, his eyes squinting like he has just woken up, struggling to focus. He starts waving at the screen.

Frantically. Is he… trying to get my attention?

He can't be, it's not real Jeff. It's like my brain mixed reality and the game together, already. Just because the character has all of Jeff's features. I tell myself to stop being silly, that AI can make anything look real. Pushing aside the unsettling feeling crawling up my spine, I click on his face. Nothing happens.

So, I guess I cannot edit his appearance. Not that I want to. But when I click his chest, a menu slides in from the right.

Jeff - "Game Jeff" - turns his head and looks at it too. His eyes widen in shock.

The menu displays a list of clothing options: t-shirts, button-ups, jumpers, suit jackets…But these aren't just any clothes.

They're Jeff's clothes.

The ones he wears to work, including the gross bright coloured floral shirt he wears on "Fun" Fridays.

I stare at the screen, fingers hovering over my mouse.

How the hell does this game know that?

It only had a picture. This is too detailed. Each time I select one, Jeff reacts. Nods in approval. Frowns in disappointment, when I don't pay attention to his reactions.

Through all of this, game Jeff, keeps waving at the screen in urgency, getting more frantic. I ignore him, although it's slowly annoying the fuck out of me. Just keep still, I am trying to concentrate.

For his party look, I chose the exact outfit he wore to last year's Christmas party.

I double check everything to make sure I am happy with the options I have chosen. I had hoped I would have more of a selection, not just Jeff's clothes. I wanted to dress him up in a hotdog suit or just have him walk around naked with his tiny penis on show. It wouldn't allow me to just leave him naked.

I click **Save**.

The screen shifts.

A town map appears. There are little houses of all sizes, Blocks of flats, bungalows, terraced houses, cottages.

There is even a shopping centre, police station, fire station, hospital, gym, library, cinema, a few little parks. There are little people going by there every-day life. I feel like I am God looking down on all of them, in total control of how their lives exist from now on. The only establishment that is missing is an airport.

I think I am going to like this world, so many options to explore, so many people to mess with.

Not just the ones I create. In the bottom left corner, Jeff stands there. Still looking bewildered. I click on a few houses.
Nothing happens.
Then I spot an icon in the top right, a hammer. I hover over it.
A tooltip appears: **Build**. I click it.
A question pops up:
What type of house do you want to have?

Three options appear:
Town House. Terraced House. Bungalow.

I chose **Townhouse**

Next question:
How many bedrooms do you want?
Options:
1. 3. 12.
I click **12**.

I plan to create a lot of people.

Next:
Do you want a basement or Attic?
I click **Basement**

The game's slogan made all sorts of scenarios fly through my head. I want this game to make my imagination come to life. My darkest thoughts.

I exit the build section.

Click Jeff. Drag him to an empty plot. His arms wave, his eyes bulge as he drops down into the world.

When he lands, he grabs his chest and doubles over like he is going to pass out.

I love the realism in this game. I notice an icon that looks like an eye. It lets me see from Jeff's point of view.

I clicked it.

Suddenly, I am staring at the floor. I laugh to myself; Jeff is not having a wonderful time.

I zoom back out. Start exploring the town. That is when I see it.

A massive house. I hover over it. The name appears:

The Controlled House.

The description reads:

"Twelve-bedroom house. Three bathrooms. Two living rooms. And a basement."

Is this the house I just created with those questions? Because if it is, then they've taken it right out of my imagination!

It is perfect. I click the icon that looks like a moving van it zooms in. The pixels form slowly. Now I am inside. The rooms automatically have lights in, which I am thankful for, to fill all the rooms with lights would have been a massive headache. It has plonked me inside the house, in the entrance part, I try to look around the rest of the house in zoom-in mode, I cannot move though apparently without a character. An error keeps popping up.

Movement can't be made, please try again with your character

I click the person icon in the corner. Jeff's face appears.

"Do you want to move Jeff to the Controlled House?"
Options:
Yes or No.
I click **Yes.**

Jeff appears in the house. He looks around. Waves at me. I swear I see his mouth move. Did he just say, *"What the fuck?"*

I stare at the screen in shock. He cannot have. He is just a game character. Right?

I need to make Jeff a bedroom in this beautiful house, just to see how this game works. There must be away of editing the building itself. I look around the screen trying to find an icon that allows me to. I find it, next to the hammer, there is a pencil, when I hover it, it says edit building. I click it,

An overlay appears over the house. Suddenly there is a grid on the layout. Okay...Now to find the smallest room in the house, I click on one, To the left of a screen a menu appears.

The words:
Garden
Living Room
Bedroom
Kitchen
Bathroom
Pets

I click **bedroom**, a new menu slides out. A small outline of a bedroom appears, interesting, I click each little outline of the furniture, each one brings up different options.

It is hard to see in the room with the walls up, I wonder if I can collapse them. I slide my mouse over and hover-over the walls, it lights up, which

usually means in other games, I have played that
I am able to do something. I click one of the
walls;
A menu pops up
Remove
Move
Collapse
Paint
I select **collapse**

A new pop-up shows
All walls or Singular wall?
I click **All walls**

All the walls collapse, perfect, I see clearly now
the space with which I am working with.
   I am going to give him the most basic, dead
bed there is. He doesn't deserve comfort!
I click the beds section again. I scroll through the
hundreds of bed options. Then I see it! A murphy
bed.
   If you have not seen a Murphy bed before,
it's a frame bed that folds up into a frame that
looks like part of your wall. Usually, they can be
quite clunky and faulty. Also, extremely
uncomfortable. I had to sleep on one when I first
moved at my mom's. The bed frame was

ridiculous, the mattresses that comes with the bed are always thin. So thin you can feel the frame underneath you.
Poor Jeff, not!

I select the **Murphy bed** drag it into the room, it snaps against the wall automatically. Nice! I then go back to the menu and select on the "**Chest of Drawers**" outline. I am just going to put a basic one in; he does not need anything special. I see one that looks like a cheap Ikea white four drawer deep chest of drawers with silver handles. You know the ones; every basic person has them. It is like the starter kit for Ikea bedroom furniture.

I press the play button to see if Jeff will react to his new room when I ask him to walk there. He goes to the room. I zoom in. He just looks constantly in shock or afraid.

The Murphy bed is folded up.

I click it, a menu pops up:
Fold down.

Leave alone.

I ask Jeff to fold it down. He walks over. I watch him jump up to grab the bar at the bottom of the bed. He pulls down with all his might. It goes down, then pulls back up before he can get it to touch the ground.

I see the frustration on his little face, By the third time the bed is down, he looks exhausted, red in the face. Is that also sweat I, see? I zoom in, sure enough there are little beads of sweat dripping down his forehead. Who knew Jeff was so unfit. I hover over the door to his room, it lights up like the walls did earlier, I click it, the options
Lock
Only Jeff can go inside
Remove
I click **Lock.**

I laugh to myself, seeing him struggle was the best part of my day, knowing he won't be able to leave this room as well. I look at the clock on the computer it is 11:11pm, how did it get so late so quickly? Better close the game down, try to sleep so I don't end up passing out on my keyboard at work. I don't need Carol having something else to moan at me about.

Chapter Seven
Ghost Signal

I watch the screen go black. Lucky for me, my bed's right behind me, so all I have to do is push my chair back and fall onto it.

My head's racing with ideas. There are so many things I can do in the game.

I can build.

I can create people.

Make them look *exactly* like their real-life counterparts. Mind blowing.

I got a bargain with this game. I grab my diary from under my pillow, write down all the ideas I have for Jeff in the game. Next thing I know, sunlight is streaming through my window. I must have fallen asleep.

I hadn't even changed into my pyjamas.

Didn't make food for work.

Didn't do anything except obsess.

Guess I'll just have to grab something on the way. I throw on my work clothes. Trousers. Not a skirt. The last thing I need is giving Jeff another reason to be a creep. Not like he needs encouragement.

The thought of in-game Jeff. Stuck there, in that pitiful room I created for him.
I can't wait for the day to be over. I've already got the next scenario planned. Oh, just you wait, Jeff. You won't be expecting this.
On the way to work, I grab a tuna and sweetcorn mayo sandwich meal from Tesco, tuna because I know Jeff hates the smell of it, it sometimes stops him from coming to my desk, a packet of ready salted crisps, and an energy drink. The only caffeine I trust.
I make it to my desk with five minutes to spare. Of, course, that's not enough for Carol. She stomps over, her face set in that permanent scowl.

"Susie, what time do you call this? We've been over this before. You need to be at your desk fifteen minutes before your shift starts."
I nod.
Press the **power button** on my computer tower.
I try to ignore her long enough that she evaporates. Only…My computer doesn't turn on. The usual green light stays dead.
I frown.

Check the cables.
Tower.
Screen.
Sockets.
Everything is plugged in. Everything looks right.
Everyone else's computers are fine, so it's not a
power thing.

"Oh, for fuck's sake,"
I mutter under my breath.

If this thing doesn't turn on, I'll have to call IT.
Which means... Jeff. Of course, it fucking does.
Every department has their own IT guy. Section
13's is Jeff. Knowing my luck, he did this on
purpose especially as he isn't hovering already
at my desk.
I might sound paranoid but believe me I feel on
edge when he isn't at my desk some days,
because I wonder what he is planning, what he
is telling people. Then he pops out of no-where I
panic. It's my natural state around him now.
   It got to the point that when errors occurred on
my computer, I taught myself basic fixes, just so
that I didn't have to call him. Watched YouTube
tutorials.
Carol's still looming. I, force a tight smile.

"Is there anything else, Carol?"

I ask her, breathing in deeply to not lose my shit at her.

"If there's something wrong with your computer, you will need to talk to Jeff"
Like I don't already know this, Carol stating the obvious as usual.

"This is why you should be here early, Susie. Now you won't be working when we start paying you."

She huffs so hard spit flies out, landing close to my Monster can, I roll my eyes and move it from spits reach. The moment anything lands in my Monster it's game over for Carol.

She's had it out for me ever since her husband, George, one of the CEOs of the Litterium, called me up to his office to applaud me on my conversion rates. My job consists of answering the phones to speak with potential Authors who want help publishing their books. I offer them our price lists, then set them up an account. That year that George called me into the office, I had hit the highest conversion rate, and I deserved the praise, but didn't deserve the little extra he tried to give.

George may be a slime ball, but he is very attractive for a man his age. Whereas Carol, she's got that stiff ear length bob, that face that's always twisted like she's smelled something rotten, and those dull brown eyes that never blink. Always in the same cheap skirt suits that hang off her making her look like a saggy bag. I swear, if George just gave her some, she wouldn't be such a miserable cow. I follow the wires to the main switchboard. Everything is on. No faults. I unplug the back cable.
Plug it back in. Press the power button again.
Nothing.
Fine!
I admit defeat.
I must call Jeff. I pick up my desk phone. Dead, of course.
Fantastic.
Now I must ask Linda next to me to use hers.

"Hey, Linda, sorry, my phone and computer are both dead. Mind if I use yours to call Jeff?"

Linda nods timidly, I walk round to her desk, I grab her phone and dial Jeff's extension 111.
It rings.
Ten times.
No answer. Then, finally, a deep voice mumbles on the other end. Not Jeff's slimy voice.

"Hello, Jeff's phone."

Weird. This is the first time anyone has ever answered Jeff's phone for him.

"Hey, is Jeff there? My whole setup isn't working in Section 13. I need him up here to take a look."

A pause. I look at the phone to make sure it's still connected

"Uh… Jeff? He hasn't turned up today. We haven't heard from him either. I'll have to come up instead. That's okay?"

Something prickles at the back of my neck. Jeff's not in? Jeff. The guy who never takes a day off. Who'd call in if he was sick.
I hesitate.

"…Yeah. Sure. I'm at desk 11."
I hang up and stare at my blank screen.
Nothing to worry about, it's just a coincidence that I made him in the game, that it looked exactly like him, and now he isn't in work. Just pure coincidence…. He will call in sick later.

The guy covering for Jeff arrives at my desk ten minutes later. He's tallish, clean-cut, with blue eyes and tanned skin. My stomach does a little flip, damn his handsome. I feel my face heating as he gives me a wave and a smile. Pull yourself together woman.

"Hi, I'm Alexander. I usually work in Section 27, but since Jeff's not in, I'll be helping you out."

He pauses, frowning slightly.

"Weird though, huh? He still hasn't called in. That's not like him."

I nod, telling myself to speak words. Any words. But I can't. For two reasons: One, I'm worried about Jeff for once, only because I am getting shivers down my spine. I made him in the game last night, but today he isn't in. I know it's probably my paranoia kicking in. But something screams at me something is wrong.
Two, this man makes my legs go to jelly.

"Right, okay, let me check you out"

I freeze. He did not just say that?
Oh. Wait.
He's talking about the computer.

I want someone to pay attention to me, it has been such a long time since I have felt anything towards anyone, I was thinking of becoming a nun at this point. But seeing Alexander definitely, makes me realise I am very attracted to the opposite sex, they just need to not be douche bags, or at least not look like one. I look down, and he is on his knees, in front of me, I am sitting on my chair, he is at the perfect height to...
Oh. Oh no
My temperature spikes, and before I can stop myself, my brain decides to play what-if scenarios. What if he, grabbed me by my hips, slid my trousers down, my knickers going with, and pulled me towards him. No! Abort. I can't be thinking this at work!
I clear my throat, trying to act normal, adjusting myself so I am sitting straight.

"Hey, Erm, I need you to move so I can check underneath."
He shouts up at me, his eyes locking onto mine.

Oh god. Oh no. I just sat there having a naughty daydream, not even thinking of what I might have looked like staring down at him. Fuck, I hope my face didn't portray what I was thinking.

"Oh, God. Yeah, sorry"
I mumble, grabbing my Monster and standing up, walking to the other side of the desk so I'm safely out of his damn way.
Then I notice Carol. She's in her office, watching me. Full-on staring.
 When I meet her eyes, she lifts a hand, wiggling her index finger at me like I'm some misbehaving schoolchild. Can she tell from there what I thinking? Or is she just assuming as usual? God, she riles me up. Stupid cow.
Meanwhile, Alexander is still under my desk. For another ten minutes. Eventually, he slides out, brushing off his hands.
"Erm, so… weirdly, your computer is missing a fuse. No idea how that happened. Did your computer work fine yesterday?"
I look at him confused.

"Yeah. It was fine."

A fuse. Missing.
Did Jeff take it? So, he could come back and fix it later, play the hero? I bet he has missed announcing to the office.

"There you go, Susie, I've fixed your computer"
He used to do it all the time, make it into a big
thing, when really, he is just doing his job.
Alexander exhales.

"Alright. I'll run downstairs and grab one."
He pauses, then turn back.

*"I know this is an odd thing to ask, and I should
do it myself, but I thought, as you two are close,
would you mind calling Jeff while I'm gone? Just
in case he's around?"*

What? What makes him think that me and Jeff
are close? What has Jeff been saying to
everyone?
I hesitate, but nod. I don't want to make it
awkward between me and Alexander by
correcting him.

"I need his number; I don't have it." I announce.

Alexander, looks at me baffled, takes his mobile
phone out of his pocket. I watch him go through
his contacts, until Jeff's name appears on his
phone.

"Just get the number off my phone and I'll be back soon, okay?"

I take the phone, gripping it tighter than necessary as I watch him disappear down the hall. No way am I calling Jeff, off my phone. I will use Alexander's. My heart pounds against my ribs as I press call.

It'll be fine. Jeff will pick up. He'll be confused as hell to hear my voice and he will just be in bed,
with a cold or migraine. Only… when the call connects, I don't hear the ringing tone. I hear that tone. The hollow Robotic out-of-area dial tone. Like his phone isn't in the UK anymore. Like Jeff isn't here anymore. I swallow hard. Where the hell is Jeff?

Chapter Eight
Execute: Isolation Protocol

The travel back home is nothing special, I wish it had been quicker though, the itch to play the game just kept building as the day went on. Alexander saying the fuse from my computer was gone, kept playing in my head, I could imagine Jeff taking it out, all smug, thinking it would make him better in my eyes, he would be "saving my day."

Then when I went into my Facebook messages when I was travelling home, I clicked on Jeff's name, to see if he had messaged. It was playing on my mind that no one had heard from him. I accidentally scrolled upwards on the message thread. There was one from the Christmas work night.

"Susie, tonight was fantastic, I love the smell of you and can't wait to have your body underneath me again."

The red mist appeared in my head, the image of him dying slowly, painfully. I get to my building, which is a high-rise of flats. I am on the top floor, which is ridiculous, but there is a lift, thank God.

So far this has not broken down. I am going to hate the day it does because I am betting there is about 10,000 steps to get to my flat or maybe I am being dramatic. I get into the lift, it ascends slowly.

I tap my foot, my impatience building, then there is a ting to say get out, I step out, the interior of this building is not the best. The walls are covered in graffiti, parts of the wall are caved in, not even sure how, they were like it when I moved in. My door itself has dent in a shape of a foot. I guess you would say this area of town is the rough side. There are a few druggies in the building, families, and it can get super loud when the children break up for school holidays.

My section though, seems to be for the lonely people. Shoved at the top where no-one can bother us, which I am grateful for. I get to my door, number 666, I laughed when I first saw the number when I viewed the place, it was fitting, because my thoughts are a little devilish. I also consume the "devils" energy drink apparently, there was an article online years ago about a woman who claimed, the M in Monster symbolises Satan, she argued that the individual three lines, is the Hebrew letter Vav, which corresponds to the sixth letter in the Hebrew alphabet, which corresponds to the number 6, making the symbol 666. Mad how much people go into detail on random details like that. I think Satan/The Devil secretly is a good guy anyway; he punishes the people who have done terrible things in their life. Just like Batman, Superman and all the other super vigilantes in comics. Everyone loves them. So, it must make them good guys, right?

I slide the key into my door and push the door hard to open it. It sometimes sticks, which can be a pain when you really need the toilet. Why is it the moment your bladder knows you are so close to a toilet it screams at you to empty it?

I dump my stuff on the floor next to my bed, Throw my coat on the bed. Walk over to the PC, press the power button. The whir sound fills the room. Fills my chest, God I can't wait to play this. I jump around the room waiting for it to load. Then start running up and down, with my arms out. I feel of energy rushing through me. I feel a buzzing throughout my veins.

Finally, the computer loads, the beautiful icon Play with Me shines at me. I jump in the chair nearly missing it as it moves slightly. I grab the mouse and double click the right button on the icon. Everything just feels dragged out when I'm waiting for the game to load. I am feeling impatient. I need it fast! NOW! INSTANT! The menu loads, there is now an extra choice on the start menu.

Continue Game.

I click this, the fan on the computer goes wild. Loud! I hope this game doesn't make my computer finally give up. I watch as pixel by pixel the game appears. It shows the map again. It's raining in the game. Weirdly, it's raining in real life to. I hear the pitter patter of the rain hitting my window ledge.

The rain sometimes calms me; it reminds me of sitting in the caravan on holiday with my parents, when things were good between us all. We used to play board games when the weather was bad on holiday. It never ruined the holiday, just meant we spent time inside, closer together. The memory swims out of my mind, as I concentrate on the game.

There is a little weather icon in the top right corner I hover it, says there is going to be a thunderstorm! How cool is it that they have their own weather to, just like they are their own country.

I quickly find the control house, click on Jeff's face in the left-hand corner. He loads into the game slowly. His head jolts from side to side, looking around in panic again. Oh, Jeff just you wait, I am going to give you something to panic about. I zoom out. I am now looking at the outer part of the house, I need to figure out how to get to the basement. I highlight over parts of the building; the foundation of the house lights up. A message pops up

Do you want to go to the basement?
Yes or No

Yes, I want to go to the basement, I click **Yes**. The view drops to the bottom floor.

I click the lights.
A carousel appears:
Turn on the lights.
Auto lights.
Change light colour.
I choose **Auto Lights**.

I select a spot in the hallway. The option "**walk here**" pops up. I select this. There is a delay, eventually Jeff begins to walk. As he passes under each light, they flicker on then off as he moves past. Creepy but cool. I am buzzing with excitement; my hands are tremble on the mouse. It hits me again, I'm controlling Jeff. Not the Jeff, but a Jeff I can do whatever I want to. I collapse all the walls. Select the **Build Tool** again.

This basement is perfect for what I have

planned, the rooms are empty so I can add items to the rooms as I wish, decorate them as I wish... Add people to them as I wish. It is about time I have some control even if it is not in real life.

I choose one of the seven rooms prebuilt in the game. I remove the lighting; I don't want Jeff to see what he is going to be walking into.

I found a fireplace in the build section under **"living room."** I drag this into the room; it snaps against the far wall. I then select a rug, it's square, looks fluffy and black. I drag this in front of the fire. That's, it. I zoom in, there is a little square box on top of the mantelpiece of the fire. It matches! Oh, the detail in this game is mind-blowing.

I switch back to Jeff control. Command him to enter the room. It's pitch black. He walks in. I wait until he is in the centre, then click Build again. I remove the door quickly. Giggling inside. A popup appears, which bursts my excitement bubble:

"Are you sure you want to do that?"
YES / NO

I frown at the computer. Why is it asking me that? It's my game. My choice. Why is it questioning me? I slam my finger on the right button of my mouse, clicking **YES.**

The message flickers, then disappears. I zoom in on Jeff's face. He looks so vulnerable. So scared. Good. At least now he feels how I did, I hope he feels trapped, that he has no control on what is happening to him. I zoom out. I yawn, my body suddenly feels drained, time to call it a night...

Chapter Nine
Dark Echoes

Jeff

I didn't want to walk into this room, it was like I had no choice, I couldn't stop my legs from moving. Someone else had control of my thoughts and actions.

A sharp pain shot through my spine, a buzzing that went through my veins, took over and now I am in total darkness.

It's so cold

Silent.

All I can hear is my breathing. I rub my hands together to keep warm. One moment there was a door, I could see it briefly, its silhouette, then I blinked, it was gone.

This is the most bizarre dream I've had. Everything that's happened so far can't be real. I must wake up soon. I'm hungry, I am tired, I need the toilet, I need to feed my rabbit. I'm trying to wake myself up, to go to the toilet, because you know what they say, you go in your dreams, then you do in real life.

I thought being in the darkness of this room was intense, it got worse, I can't see anything now. Everything has disappeared. What's going on?

I scream out, it's like the darkness swallows my voice.

I lift my hand in front of me, only I don't have one, I'm now just a conscious in this void. I feel like I'm floating. A digital count down appears in front of me, counting down from 180. I don't know what it's counting down to. There is nothing I can do; I just stare at the numbers in the void. Which occasionally flickers as the seconds go down, it makes me panic that it will disappear, it's the only form of light. I don't want to just be here in the dark. I swear when I wake up, I am going straight to a therapist, this can't be healthy. To dream of such things. The timer gets closer to 0, when it hits 10 seconds, I hear the whirring sound of a loading computer? tip tapping of a keyboard and click of a computer mouse? It echoes around the room. What the actual fuck is happening? Am I now dreaming of computers?

The room starts to transform around me, my body reappearing.

Chapter Ten
Glitches and Doppelgängers

I wake up suddenly, I am in a sweat. I had a dream that Jeff is missing from the game not just in real life. In my dream I open the game, and he's gone, never created. I need to make it was just a dream. I just need to, I check the time, it's 3am. I plunder over to the computer in my half-asleep state; I clumsily load the computer. The sound of the computer is getting worse each time I load this game. It's so loud, the neighbours probably can hear it. I hope it doesn't wake them. I don't fancy them knocking on my door.

I hold my breath as I watch Jeff appear. Phew, okay, he is still here. My thoughts are racing again, worrying if Jeff will arrive at work today and if he doesn't where is he? This isn't the real Jeff; I keep reminding myself.
Why does this Jeff look so afraid? I need to stop with the energy drinks.
I read somewhere that they can cause paranoia. It does give me a thrill to see the look on his face. As I'm awake, I may as well see if the game allows me to create one of the scenarios from my diary. I walk over to my bed and grab the diary from my pillow. I then here a PING as a

message appears up on the screen.

"Do you want to put a door in?"
 Yes or No.

Ugh, this game. I storm over to the computer mouse, If I wanted to, I would. I click **No**. The game glitches a little and carries on.
I sit back down in my computer chair, flip the pages to the entry I wrote, Jeff, Matches, Fire! I saw a few videos on TikTok of gamers who play Sims, if you put the rug next to the fire then ask the character to light it, there's a chance the rug will catch a light, then spread onto them to. I just want to see if this game has the same functions.
  The thought of Jeff on fire and in pain, makes me happy. Maybe a little too happy. I move the mouse around the room.
  The walls shine, a + sign appears above them. What does that mean? I click on it. A carousel menu appears again.
The options:
Add a door. *Nope*
Add an accelerant. *Maybe*.
Add windows. Nope
Remove walls. Nope.
 Out of those four options, I think adding an accelerant wins. I click it, expecting something to

happen. It doesn't. I look at where Jeff is. He is just there staring at his hands. How anti climatic.

In the top left corner, there is a button that says, **"free roam."** Wonder what this does? I clicked it. Suddenly, Jeff is moving around on his own. In a panic.

Chapter Eleven
Firewall Breached

Jeff

OH MY GOD, I am free from whatever was controlling me, the pain down my spine is gone, the buzz in my veins gone.

With this sense of freedom, I try to wake myself up, I've heard that pain can wake you up from dreams. Guess it's worth a shot.

I pinch my arm, hard! It stings like hell, I'm still here. In this dark, freezing room. I slap myself. Nothing. Still here. What else can I do?

I take slow, careful steps forward, feeling my way through the pitch-black room. The air feels heavy. There's barely any oxygen in here! After about twenty steps, my hands meet a wall. Rough,

Cold brick.

No wallpaper.

No plaster.

Just raw stone.

The moment my fingers brush against it, the wall lights up for two seconds, a brief, eerie glow. Then, something thick, cold, and watery begins to ooze down the bricks. My breath catches. I yank my hands back and stumble away, my pulse pounding. What the fuck was that? I look down at my hands, I forget I can't see a damn thing, I end up just wiping the liquid down myself.

I scramble along the wall, hands searching desperately for a way out. A door, a vent, anything. There's nothing. No exit. Just these endless walls, except for one thing: a fireplace, I feel its wooden mantelpiece, I bend down, I think that's ashes, the fire has been used before, I stand back up, feeling across the top of the mantel piece. My hand hits something. Matches!

The fire is dead centre on the far back wall. Did I mention I'm barefoot? I watched every other part of clothing appear on me, but no shoes, I don't even know why. They're now on the hard stone, icy and stinging. Every step feels like a fresh sting. But then softness as I back up a bit from the fireplace. Fur, maybe? A rug? It's like heaven under my aching feet.

I try not to panic, but how the hell am I supposed to stay calm?

No doors.

No food.

No water.

No toilet.

No bed.

Just a fireplace, a pack of matches, and this damn rug. What have I done to deserve this?

I shake my head. This is just a dream. Everything's fine. I'll wake up soon. Won't I?

My heart is pounding so fast I swear I can feel it slamming against my ribs. I sit down on the rug, rubbing my feet together for warmth. I can't take this anymore. This room is driving me insane. I need to get out. *I need to wake up.*
Then it happens.
That same pain runs down my spine, the buzz back in my veins my control gone.

My legs force me to stand. My arms reach for the matches on the mantel. I don't want to do this! I try to stop myself, I can't. My hands shake, trying to stop this from happening, I look up, I glance up where the ceiling should be.

Instead, I see Susie. It's as though I'm in a little doll house of hers, only she is sitting down on a computer desk. Behind her, her bed. I can see a fridge in a corner, shelves of books.

She's looming over me like a giant, grinning too wide, her face stretched and distorted.

I can't scream. My fingers close around the matchbox. I pull one out and strike it against the rough side. It dies out. Phew.
Another one. Snuffed out.
But my hands won't stop. I crouch in front of the fireplace. Another match.

It stays lit.

Oh, fuck.

I watch, helpless, as my body places it in the fire.

I am panicking because earlier when I touched inside the fire, I swear I could smell some type of lighter fluid. If this lights…

Boom!

Fire explodes.

Bits of embers go everywhere onto the rug. It goes up in flames. I try to move to pat the fire out, but I still don't have control of my body. The pain sharpens the moment I try to move.

It gets worse.

The walls around the rug ignite into flames. The whole room is a firebox.

I'm so hot. I feel sweat go down my neck, down my palm. I wipe my lip as sweat appears there.

That's when I smell it.

Gasoline!

I'm covered in gasoline! It must have been on the walls. That must have been the liquid I wiped down myself...

BOOM!

The fireplace explodes again. Embers sear my skin.

Fire.

Heat.

Pain.

I'm burning. The agony is excruciating. Why am I

not waking up?

Please.

Someone.

Help me.

I can't breathe.

A scream rips from my throat. A sound I've never made before.

I've never had a reason to. But this pain? It's unlike anything I've ever felt.

My heart pounds, frantic, as flames consume me. I try to move, to roll, to put myself out but I can't.

Susie or whatever is still controlling me, won't release me. I stay frozen in place, helpless as the fire devours me. My chest tightens, the smoke thick in my lungs. This isn't how I thought it would end.

Not like this.

Chapter Twelve
Error 404: Jeff Not Found

I watch as Jeff screams in pain. For a moment, my own heart stops. It sounds so real. I remind myself this is just a game. I'm not actually killing the real Jeff.

Still, I turn the volume down. Just in case the neighbours hear.

As his body writhes, the fire consuming him, I laugh. He deserves this. For every woman he's ever extorted. Every threat. Every sick grin.

Then, a notification pops up.
"Error 404: Jeff Not Found."

What?
I press **OK**.
The screen refreshes.
Jeff's body is gone.
A glitch? Or he was just... removed after dying? How bizarre. I check around the basement, in the other six rooms, nothing, I check the upper half of the building again, nothing. Has the game just removed him because he died?

I smirk. I'm not making him again. That was exactly how I imagined it.

PART TWO

ESCALATION

Chapter Thirteen
Echoes of the Game

That night was a restless sleep, I had images of Jeff going up in flames, how he screamed, how realistic it sounded. I woke up with my clothes stuck to me, my temperate high. I kept reminding myself it's just a game, Real life Jeff is fine, living his best life being a creep. Probably sleeping soundly in his bed.

It didn't help me either that every time I tried to sleep, I kept hearing the whirr of the computer as if it was trying to load something, even though I had closed it fully down. I checked several times, I was very tempted to rip the plug out the back, I didn't because of how old the computer is, I was worried it would break completely.

Morning soon appears and I'm back at my desk. When handsome Alexander peers over my screen, I am half asleep. Not registering that he shouldn't be here.

"Hi, how you are doing?"
He asks with a smile across his gorgeous face, his eyes slightly lighting up but there's also a dim of worry across his face

"Oh Hi, I am fine thanks, computers running like a charm now, You, okay?"
I ask with concern in my voice. Well, I hope it is portrayed that way. Sometimes I don't know what tone of voice to use in certain circumstances.

"Yeah Man, I'm fine, although Jeff still hasn't appeared for work, I keep trying to call him, but that weird tone keeps blaring down the phone. Last night, I swore I heard a whisper of a voice, or I'm just losing it."
he rambles

"A voice? What did it say?"

I'm getting concerned about Jeff myself, I have had no message from him, usually by now he would have visited my workstation several times. What if? What I did? No, it couldn't have. It's a game remember.

"Yeah, a voice man, it sounded so eerie. It said something like Play with Me, I thought it was Jeff mucking around, but when I looked at my phone, it said no one has answered"

I try to keep my cool. Even though internally I am

panicking to high heaven, why is Jeff's phone not working and how did Alexander hear the name of the game through Jeff's phone? This can't be happening. It's all just a coincidence, right?

"Has anyone been around Jeff's to see if he is, okay?" I ask.

"Honestly, No, no one has, but that's a good call, I think I will pop by after work"
Alexander exclaims

Just as he is about to leave, we both notice a guy in a suit leaving Carol's office, looking all professional. Who could he be? New person starting? Only when we see Carol's face she is crying. Literally full of tears rolling down her face. In the five years I have worked with Carol, I've never seen Carol cry. Something serious must have happened. Everyone now has all eyes on the front of the room.

    The man stands with Carol outside her office, I see her take a few deep breaths, before turning to all of us. The tension in the air is thick, waiting for her to say something. She grabs a tissue from her pocket, dabs at her eyes.

"Everyone, can I have your attention?"
She announces to the room, her voice cracking. Everyone stops typing, I hear some of them turn the ring down on their phones.

"This is Detective Verum, he is from the homicide department. He will need to ask you all a couple of questions. I will let him take over now and explain."
She looks down at her feet.

   A homicide detective? What the fuck? Why is he here? I am sure everyone is thinking the same, I have nothing to worry about, I keep saying to myself. This is nothing to do with…
The detective words cut through my thoughts.

"Yes, as Mrs. Mendex has said, I'm here to investigate a homicide that recently happened. Last night, Mr. Sinclair's body was found two miles from here. I can't disclose the matter fully, but we would like to establish a timeline on when Mr. Sinclair was last seen."

   My stomach hollows. Jeff's dead? What are the odds of this? I killed him only last night in the game. He disappeared from it when it happened. It can't have been me. It is only a game! I try to calm my breathing. I can't hyperventilate right now; people will see it as suspicious. Then again... would they? I am "close" to Jeff, according to him and everyone else in this fucking building.

"Mrs. Mendex has created a list of people who have worked closely with Mr. Sinclair. This doesn't mean we are accusing you. So don't panic."

 He calls the first name. it's not me. I release the breath I hadn't realised I was holding. The detective had called Bob, he used to play DND with Jeff on Fridays, then they suddenly stopped seeing each other. We all just assumed they got bored of it.
But maybe it's another reason?
   The day goes by like this, him calling people one by one. Each time my heart skips a beat wondering if it'll be me next. My name never gets called. Of course it didn't though, right?

Chapter Fourteen
Unexpected Bug

I rush home after work. I must check the game. There has got to be a way to bring Jeff back. Maybe I missed something. A previous save can fix it.

The second I am through the door, I throw my bag down and jab the power button, I can't contain my anxiousness. The machine kicks into gear, loud as usual, slow, like it is stalling on purpose.

Typical. Now it wants to drag its feet.

The screen loads.

I hesitate. My stomach hollows as I remember that Jeff is dead in real life. Do I even want to open this thing again? What's it going to achieve? At the same time, I do. I need to. I just need to know if I can bring him back. I know it won't bring real Jeff back.

I don't know how to process that Jeff is dead, I won't see him again. No more snide comments, no new messages on Facebook.

Least if I bring him back in the game, it'll give me the sense of relief that I didn't cause his death.

I double-click the "**Play with Me icon.**"

The menu blinks into view, big red house, black windows, that weird feeling like someone is watching me from the house creeps over me. I look over the house again. The colour has changed from green to red. How odd. Is it angry at me? For what I've done? This game makes me think of the craziest things.

My eyes track over the menu options. The "**Load Game**" choice is gone!

Just… "**Start New.**"

What?

No. That is not right.

I saved the game. I know I did.

I try not to cry, I feel it building in me, I am full on panicking.

Why do I even care that Jeff's gone? I hated him. I missed how we were together, not the person he turned out to be. I back out of the game, go digging through the system.

"**My Computer**" right-click, **Properties**, **Earlier Versions**…

There it is 10PM. Proof I was in the game.

So where the hell is the save file?

I reloaded the game.

Still nothing. No Jeff.

No saved data.

Just a fresh start, like nothing ever happened.

Maybe the game can't register something
that's... gone.
Like it is wiped clean because Jeff's doesn't exist
anymore.
I burst into tears, this isn't how it was meant to
go. Let's try again.

Chapter Fifteen
New player Entered.

It doesn't matter who I choose, nothing will happen. They will still exist in the real world. That's what I keep telling myself as I hold my breath and click **Create New Player**.

I think I'm going to create Carol because her constant breathing down my neck pisses the fuck out of me, the way she looked at me when Alexander was at my desk as well! Who the fuck is she to judge me?

Especially when she never comforted me through what happened with Jeff at the Christmas party. She was there when I ran into the toilet. She asked what was wrong, I told her with tears streaming down my face, trembling, trying to get my breathing regulated. She had the audacity to blame me. Said if I wore something "*less revealing*" or wasn't "*so friendly*" with men, then it wouldn't have happened.

That soon stopped me crying because I was in shock, another woman had said that to me.

I wasn't even dressed provocatively.

I was wearing a damn trouser suit, for Christ's sake.

Yes, I'm friendly with men. We just get along better. I'm a gamer, I eat like a man, hell, you could say I act like one too.

How she treated me after the George incident too. URGH!

Yeah it must be fucking Carol. Stupid bitch.

This time, I'm ready. Last year's work-do photo already has her in it, no need to crawl through Facebook's black hole again. I upload the image, just like clockwork, she flickers into view, confused, blinking like she's been dropped in the middle of a crime scene. Her eyes are bulging, judgmental, that same goddamn look she gives when someone dares to talk while she's talking to the room. I dress her quickly, nothing fancy, just enough to wipe the smugness off her pixelated face. Honestly, I couldn't dress her fancy anyway with her out-dated clothes. Then I drag her down to the basement.

The second she drops, her arms flail like a puppet on invisible strings. I giggle. I don't mean to, but I do. Watching her scramble like that? It's makes me feel better. Less panicked. No, wait. I want to see what happens if I create two people. Can they live in the same save?

Someone's got to live in this massive building, right? The top half, at least. Not the basement. Obviously.

Let's see… I scan the screen, eyes darting

around for the **"Create Character"** button.
Sure enough, when I hover over an icon of a
stick figure, a message pops up:
"Create another person?"
I clicked it.
The usual character creation screen loads.
Now, who to make?
Carol's husband?
After all, he is the reason Carol hates my guts.

He's the one who slid his hand up my leg while
talking to me in his office, walked around his
desk, crouched right in front of me, and
just…started creeping his hands up my thigh like
it was nothing. I was about to shove my chair
back, send him flying when Carol walked in.
Sees him, hands on me and what does she do?
Screams at *me*. Of course. Because it's my fault,
not her wandering-hands husbands. I looked at
her in disbelief. This was before the Jeff incident,
so I didn't know how she'd react.

Of course George, the guy who created the
definition of Gas lighter, played innocently,
claiming I egged him on by the way I looked at
him. "*I'm a man,*" he said. "*I can't help myself*"

If there was ever a moment in my life where I
wanted to grab the letter opener off someone's
desk, slice the metal across their neck, it was

that moment. And to be honest? I still wish I had. People with money act like they're untouchable. The wives don't dare contradict them, scared of losing the house, the job, the whole fake little life they built. I'm supposed to feel sorry for Carol. I don't. We all have choices.
Screw it. George it is.

I use the same photo from Christmas. The game makes him quickly. I dress him in whatever's clothes that's loaded from his wardrobe, this time when I press save, the game gives me a choice:

What's George's relationship to Carol?
Siblings.
Married.
Strangers.
Let's see what happens when I make them strangers…

Chapter Sixteen
Load Complete

Carol

Jesus H. Christ! Where am I? I was just closing the office, then I felt this weird, fuzzy electric buzz wash over me. Everything went black. It felt like I had closed my eyes for eternity. When I eventually opened them. I'm standing on some kind of platform, in front of a mirror, there's this giant version of Susie just… staring down at me.

I was mortified. I looked down and I was naked! I must've passed out or I must be hallucinating. The pills I take, can make reality a bit out of sorts sometimes. I haven't hallucinated on them though, I know it's one of the side effects the doctors warned me about though. This must be what's happening. Not sure why it's created the scenario of Susie controlling me though.

Could it be my subconscious heightening my feelings towards her? Finding out Jeff is dead, made me think about how Susie cried when he sexually assaulted her. How I wasn't much of a comfort to her. I literally thought about it as I was entering the key into the lock at work. Now here I am stuck, Susie looming over me. When I tried to look up at her again though, darkness took over me. I can't see my body. Can't feel anything. Just hear my thoughts.

Chapter Seventeen
He Glitched First

George

Must've drank too much again waiting for Carol to come home. I have to drink to even look at her these days. She's let herself go, forty years together, the only thing that's grown is my hatred for her.

I must've passed out. One minute I'm on the sofa, the next blackness. Then I wake up in front of a mirror, on a platform. No idea how I got here and for some reason I am fucking naked!
Just staring at my knob in the mirror.

Chapter Eighteen
Patch 1.18: New Characters Loaded

That wasn't the sight I wanted to see when I loaded George into the game.
I full-on forgot they load in naked.
Even Jeff had better junk than George.
He has a hairy Dad bod, topped off with a lifeless miserable penis. Honestly, why do men think their penis is attractive? His looks like it would never stand to attention. I rushed to dress him, desperate to erase the image from my mind before it seared itself into my nightmares. Once clothed, barely. I placed him beside Carol in the mansion. They looked at each other. I leaned closer to the screen, squinting.
Did I just see that? A flicker of... panic? Recognition?
No way. The realism in this game catches me off guard sometimes, I can't lie.
Let's see if these two are into each other. There must be some kind of relationship mechanic in this game. They wouldn't give me the possibility to pair them if it didn't, right?

For now, I'm still controlling George. Who is currently spinning in circles, slapping his arms against his sides, and huffing like a madman.

Carol just watches him. Silent. Her expression

twisted in pure disgust. If this were real life, I swear Carol would be thinking, What the fuck did I marry?

And honestly? Fair.

Chapter Nineteen
Click to Violate

I tried everything.
I gave them romantic dinners. Gifts.
Compliments. Hell, I even made George start painting like Jack from Titanic. "Paint me, like one of your girls, George" I thought as I made Carol ask him to paint her.
Nothing worked. Every flirt failed. Every interaction ended with Carol walking away or visibly gagging.
"Carol finds George unpleasant."
"Failed attempt at romance."
"Negative sentiment gained."
She laughed at his painting, I did to, George however, went red in the face.
Blah Blah Blah
Even the game knew he was a pathetic excuse of a man, that their connection wasn't real, their marriage only existed because of how much money he had in the bank. Yet Carol had the audacity, in real life, to blame me for what he did. She sided with him. With Jeff. With all of them. I exhale, hard, staring at the screen.
 Carol is sitting on the edge of the bed upstairs, reading. George is loitering downstairs in his boxers, scratching himself like a cave dweller

The icon above his head is red. Uncomfortable, unhappy. Pathetic. Good. I don't want him to be happy; He doesn't deserve to be.
I click on George.
Then click on Carol.
A list of interactions pops up.
Talk
Joke
Insult
Fight
Flirt (greyed out)
Compliment (greyed out)
Do the Deed (greyed out)
I click do the **Deed** anyway.

Pop-up:
Warning: No romantic connection exists between these characters.
Proceeding may result in permanent emotional damage and unstableness.
Are you sure you want to continue?
YES / NO
My hand hovers over the mouse. I remember Carol's voice:

"Maybe if you didn't dress like that, things wouldn't have happened."

Condescending, little whiney voice.
I remember her standing at the sink, staring at
me like I was a problem, not a victim.

"You were always too friendly with the men."
My finger twitches.

*"He's your manager, Susie. You misunderstood
his intentions."*

I close my eyes.
Click. **YES.**
The screen flickers.

Chapter Twenty
Unresponsive Player: Carol.exe

Carol

This is a nightmare. No Hallucination would last this long.

It must be a recurring nightmare.

I can't move. Can't scream. Can't wake up.

I'm in a bedroom I don't recognise. Everything's too crisp. Too clean. Like it's been built, not lived in. something worse: that feeling. That *buzz*. It starts in my spine. A painful, static crackle, electricity crawling through my nerves. I know this feeling now. It happens right before I lose control. Right before something else takes over my body.

The more I resist, the worse it gets. My muscles seize. My joints lock. My thoughts start to blur.

The door creaks.

Footsteps. Heavy. Familiar.

George enters the bedroom. He's half-dressed. Drenched in sweat. His eyes vacant but zoned on me. Like he knows exactly what he's about to do, but not why. He climbs onto the bed.

The mattress dips beneath his weight. He turns to me

I try to fight it. Scream. Anything. The electricity surges again, burning behind my eyes. My body locks up. Paralysed

His hands. On me. Heavy. Possessive.

No. This isn't happening.

It's not real. It's just a dream.

But it feels real. Too real.

I can't move.

I can't stop him.

Then I hear it. Not George. Not my own thoughts.

A laugh.

Detached. Cold. Familiar.

Susie.

She's here. Watching.

Why is this happening to me?

I try to scream it. But it's only a whisper in my head.

Chapter Twenty- One
Scripted Desire

George

She doesn't want it. I can feel it. She's stiff. Cold.
Eyes clamped shut like she's trying to disappear.
Her body doesn't respond. It's like she's not
even in there anymore.
But I keep going.
Whoever is making this happen? They're getting
what they want.
And if I'm honest?
So am I.
Something inside me snarls,
Take what's yours.
Her body should be mine. Who is she to look at
me like I'm worthless? Like I'm disgusting?
I'm the best she'll ever have.
I *deserve* this.
A pulse of static rips through my stomach. The
pain is sharp, electric.
But I don't try to stop what's happening. It just
fuels me. She's crying now. Quietly.

And *that* makes everything worse. Because I like it.

My body moves on its own. Harder. Faster. Then it's over.

And all I feel is relief.

The buzz goes in my head and the pain in my spine releases; I am now in control again.

Chapter Twenty-Two
Achievement Unlocked: Regret

I sit back.

The screen dims.

Carol curls up on the bed, rocking. George once he had finished, just left her there, exited the bedroom, started wandering the hallway like nothing happened. Like he didn't just violate his own wife. Like it was nothing more than taking a piss. I know I did that; I made it happen. I just thought when I released George from my control he would at least talk to her, see if she okay. But he didn't.

A pop-up appears:

"Emotional trauma detected. Characters may begin to experience instability."

I click **OK**.

I don't feel better.

I thought I would.

I stare at Carol's face. Her blank, broken expression.

For a second, I think I hear her voice from my speakers.

A broken cry.

"Why?"

Just one word. Tiny. Barely there. It makes my stomach twist. I close the game. The fan on my computer keeps whirring, like it's still working on something.

Something I can't undo, I know what George and Jeff did to me wasn't as bad as what I put her through. She needed to learn that men don't care what the woman are wearing, they just take, because think they can. She needed to learn. Didn't she?

PART THREE

TIGHTENING THE NOOSE

Chapter Twenty-Three
File Not Closed

I knew the nightmares would come. instead of watching George hurt Carol, I was Carol with him on top of me. I wish my brain could separate fiction from fact. What happened was fantasy, not reality. Even though it didn't seem fake. It felt like I was watching a horror movie. My heart hurts for what I did. Carol and George are fine. Living in some posh countryside house, probably eating lobster or some other pretentious meal. I imagine housekeepers serving on them hand and foot. I don't even know if they have housekeepers, it wouldn't surprise me.

The computer didn't shut down properly again last night. I kept hearing it, whirring, buzzing, while I tried to sleep. Even though I know it was shut down, I made sure of it. Once, I opened my eyes, I swear I saw a pulsing red light coming from the screen. The moment I focused, it vanished. Maybe I was in-between sleep and wake state? Still, I can't shake the feeling that the game is watching me too. I feel like I'm going insane. It's always there now. Constantly, thrumming through my head. Like I am connected to it, that thrum, is it telling me I am a part of the game to? Does that make it the greatest game ever made... or the most disturbing? I haven't decided yet.

I feel awful today. "Refreshed after poor sleep" is a joke. When I got to work, I grab a coffee instead of my usual Monster just to feel something different. There were dark grey bags under my eyes. Full-on black rings, when I looked in the mirror earlier and I was deathly pale as well. The office feels strange. Off.   The Detective's back again. I spotted him standing outside Carol's office, waiting.

Weird, considering Carol's usually the first one in. Maybe she's finally realised her husband's part-owner of the company, so she doesn't have to show up early anymore.

Chapter Twenty-Four
System Error: Coding Missing

We all continue with our work, but I swear I'm not the only one peeking over my screen every few minutes, eyes drifting to the office door. Waiting. Everyone's waiting for Carol.
This isn't a good look for her not with the Detective here. The one week she decides to be late... *Why now*? Then it happens.
The Detective's phone rings, sharp, cutting through the soft office murmur. It cuts through the silent office, like an alarm. He answers. I watch him. Intently. You can hear a voice on the other end, but not the words. Just enough to make the hair on your arms rise. His face falls. His hand scrubs down his face, trying to wipe something away maybe the news.
His eyes scan the room.
Searching.
Have they heard something? About Jeff?
I haven't been told much. Only that his body was found burned, like, scorched. Unrecognisable. That must be a coincidence. Must be. Then he moves. Straight to Linda's desk, she's our acting supervisor when Carol's off.

The call ends. He looks agitated. Tense.

He leans in and whispers,
"Can we talk in Carol's office, please?"

Linda blinks, then nods slowly, clearly confused.
My chest tightens.
What the hell is happening?
Where is Carol?
This can't be happening.

Chapter Twenty-Five
Corrupted Memory File

Carol

I'm back in the blackness, alone with only my thoughts.

But I can feel him too. George. His presence presses in around me like static, silent, but there. I don't know which part I hate more. The floating in this endless dark, where my body isn't mine and I'm nothing but a drifting thought... Or when the world starts forming again. Piece by piece. Stage by stage. Because that's when I know I'm going back. Back into a worse hell. A place where my thoughts are mine, but my memories aren't. Where I forget who I am... And who I was to George. In the void, we remember. We remember everything. Who we were outside this nightmare, how we felt, what we did.

But as soon as this whatever it is starts rebuilding itself, it all slips away. I forget George. I forget us, all I'm left with is revulsion. The way he looks at me makes my skin crawl. In the void, it's all real, real memories, real emotions, real echoes of what happened in there. Well, what feels real. I can't speak to him there. Only remember and the scariest part. The last time he hurt me in that nightmare; I saw something in him. I could tell when it was the something else pulling the strings… But I also saw him. The real him. I had never seen that version of George before. Which makes me wonder. Has he always been like this? Has he just been hiding it from me all these years? We've been together since Secondary School. Forty years. I should know him, right? I should know my own husband, only, right now, it feels like I don't. My heart is breaking, and I can't even cry out in this stupid fucking darkness.

Although all of this feels extremely real, it is the longest dream I have ever had. I just need to figure out how to get out of this. Because right now, I just want to break down. I need to break down.

It's making me question everything. I can't cope.

Chapter Twenty-Six
NPC or Player?

Everyone's eyes follow Linda as she disappears into Carol's office with the Detective. They don't think to shut the blinds.

I would have. Through the glass, we watch him gesture toward the chair. Linda hesitates, barely a pause, then sits on the edge of the seat, just like he asked.

Linda's the kind of person who wouldn't say boo to a goose. Mousy. Quiet. Soft-spoken. She gives off full cosy-grandma vibes, even though she's only in her thirties. Always polite. Always kind. Today she's in one of her handmade knitted cardigans, sage green with tiny pearl buttons, over a plain white blouse, mum jeans, and those sensible black shoes she wears every day. She looks like someone who brings banana bread to church meetings. Not someone who gets pulled into closed-door conversations with a Detective.

Chapter Twenty-Seven
Detective Verum Field Notes

Detective Verum

I wasn't expecting this today. Mr and Mrs Mendex's were supposed to meet me this morning, we had a meeting scheduled to discuss Jeff's death or rather, what I suspect may be homicide. But neither of them showed up. No call. No excuse. Nothing. That struck me as off. She at least didn't seem like the type to flake out, especially on something this serious. She gave the impression of someone who follows protocol, someone who shows up even when she's barely holding it together.

When they didn't arrive, I had one of my team check their house. Meanwhile, I went ahead with my visit to their workplace. I didn't mention they were missing. I walked in like everything was fine just to see the reactions. Sure enough, the tension was palpable.   Everyone was on edge, casting glances toward the door, waiting for Carol like she might appear at any second. The receptionist was about to start sanitising her desk again probably for the third time that morning. That's when the call came through. Mr Mendex car is still at home.

When the team looked through the windows of their house, it appeared as though he'd been drinking. Half a glass of whiskey sat abandoned on the table. When they knocked, a cleaner answered the door.

"I was dismissed last night by Mr. Mendex," she explained. *"But when I came back this morning, I had to let myself in. No one was home. I assumed they'd gone to work together they occasionally share Mrs. Mendez's car"*

They pulled CCTV from their workplace. Mrs Mendex car is still parked in the Litterium' car park. Footage from the building's main entrance shows her locking up. Then. The feed glitches. She's gone. I haven't seen the footage yet, the second I do, I know exactly what I'll feel. A cold ripple down my spine. Because it sounds exactly like what happened to Jeff.
The glitch.
The disappearance.
Like they were edited out of reality. We ran tests on Jeff. Traces of gasoline were found on his body, only, the type used doesn't exist. At least, not in any system we have access to. That alone raises questions. But what I can't shake is what

was carved into him.

Play with Me.

It wasn't handwritten. It wasn't messy.
It looked like it had been machine etched.
Precise. Surgical. Deliberate.
Whatever's happening, it's not natural and my instincts? They're screaming.

Chapter Twenty-Eight
Interview with Linda

Detective Verum

I asked Linda into Carol's office because someone needs to be told to hold the fort. Technically, she's the acting supervisor. But from the way she entered the room, small steps, shoulders hunched, you'd think I'd summoned her for a public execution.

She looks like a gust of wind could knock her flat, Fragile. Not guilty. But on the edge of unravelling, she sits when I gesture to the chair, rubbing her hands like she's trying to scrub off invisible guilt. Her cardigan sleeves are already fraying at the cuffs.

"Linda,"

I begin, careful not to sound too harsh,

"Mr. and Mrs. Mendex are currently unaccounted for. We haven't been able to reach either of them.
No calls. No texts. Nothing."

She blinks. Stares at me like I've just spoken in another language.

"What? No, I, I haven't heard from Carol. That's not like her. She's always on time. And if she needed me to cover for anything, she'd tell me. Even if it was something stupid like running late from traffic."

"When was the last time you saw her?"

"Yesterday. Just before five. We spoke briefly in the hallway; she was muttering about someone leaving the printer jammed again... I said goodnight and that was it."

"You didn't see her leave?"
She shakes her head.

"No. she always locks up. It's her thing. She checks every light, every door, every plug socket. She was putting the key in the door when I left."

I raise an eyebrow.

"So, you did see her at the front door?"

"Yeah. She had just turned the key in the lock. I didn't think anything of it. I waved; she waved back. I assumed she got in her car and left."
I nod slowly, my pen stilling over my notepad.

"Security confirmed she locked the front door at 5:06 PM. The CCTV shows her inserting the key, then stepping back to check the handle."
Linda looks up at me.

"Okay…?"

"That's when the footage glitched."
I mumble to myself more than to Linda. Her eyes widened.

"What do you mean glitched?"

"Oh, sorry you weren't meant to hear that. In the footage she was there and the next, she wasn't. Like someone sliced the frame in half and edited her out."

Linda's lip quivers.

"Oh god… so she's really gone?"

She doesn't wait for an answer. She breaks. Crying hard now, ugly, full-body sobs that shake her frame like she's trying to mourn something she hasn't even been allowed to process yet.

I let her cry. I never know what to do when people start crying out of nowhere, I just sit there awkwardly waiting for it to stop. My mind wanders off, this case, it's blowing my mind. People don't just vanish. Not like that.

Chapter Twenty-Nine
Internal Systems Overheating

Oh my god.
Why is Linda crying?
My heart slams against my ribcage like it's trying
to escape. No. No, no, no. This isn't happening
again. This can't be another Jeff incident. It's just
a coincidence. It must be. Everything's fine. I
didn't do anything. It's just a game

The office is dead silent as the door creaks
open. Linda steps out with the Detective. Her
face is blotchy, her eyes red, and I can still see
the tear tracks on her cheeks. She doesn't say
anything at first. She just stands there, twisting
her fingers.
Everyone stares. No one breathes. Even the
keyboards stop clacking. Then, finally, she
speaks. Barely above a whisper.

*"Hi, everyone. As you may have noticed, Carol
hasn't come into work today.
Now, we're not sure where she or George are.*

The Detective will be staying for a while. If anyone knows anything, or… saw anything strange, please come forward."

She shuffles to her desk like she's made of glass and afraid someone might bump into her and shatter her completely.
The second she sits, the whispering starts.
Quiet. Rapid. Office gossip feeding on fear like it always does. And me? I'm just trying not to pass the fuck out. I can feel it. The panic crawling up my throat like it wants to choke me. My fingers are twitching. My eyes are wide Act natural, Susie. Breathe. Breathe, damn it.
Would I be sad? Is that the vibe I'm meant to give off?
Everyone *knows* Carol and I didn't get along.
So what's appropriate here, confused? Concerned? Mildly annoyed?
Do NOT look excited, Susie. I feel like I'm hyperventilating.
I grab my water bottle with a hand that's not shaking (okay, yes, it is) and take a sip. Try to steady my breathing Name five things you can see. The stapler, The flickering monitor.
The post-it note that says "Smile, it's Monday."
Linda's cardigan. My Monster can. Good. Good.
That's five. Now breathe.
This isn't my fault.

It's not.

It's just…weird timing.

Coincidence.

Tomorrow we'll hear from them. They'll call in, saying they went on a spontaneous couples' retreat. Something romantic and totally out of character.

"You only live once," right?

Because if this is what I think it is then I've got bigger problems than pretending to be sad.

Chapter Thirty
Corrupted Files & Shaky Justifications

At this point, I'm even getting tired of rushing home like I care.

Because I don't. Not really.

I don't care about these people.

I never have.

Here I am. Practically sprinting for the bus, heart hammering, thoughts racing. Why?

I don't even know what I'm expecting. Maybe I think if I repeat what I did to Jeff, Carol and George will come back.

Reverse it. Undo it.

Like the game's some kind of twisted ctrl+Z button for reality.

I burst through my front door and dropped my bag without bothering to shut it. I don't even take off my shoes. I just go straight to the computer and jab the power button.

It flashes red.

Of course it does.

Same as always.

I don't even wait this time.

As soon as it loads, I slam my finger down on mouse, the arrow cursor on the Play with Me icon. Double click.

But I don't stick around.

No watching the house flicker into view. No admiring the creepy title screen.

I'm going to make toast.

Open a packet of crisps.

Crack open a drink.

Because if I don't distract myself, I'll claw my own skin off.

By the time I get back, the screen's glowing.

That *buzzing* in my skull is back.

Faint at first. Then louder. Like a TV left on in another room but *inside my brain*.

And now…

there's a **Load Game** button. At least the save is still there I guess

I click it.

The loading bar crawls across the screen like it's in pain. Slower than usual.

Juddering. Glitching. Like it doesn't want to open this file.

The buzzing intensifies. Like a swarm of bees trapped behind my eyes.

I squeeze them shut, press my knuckles to my temples, take a deep breath.

It's fine.

I open them again.

The game is loaded.

Oh god.

Carol!

She's standing in the hallway.

There's something wrong with her.

Her body is splinched like she glitched mid loading.

Her torso is angled one way, her legs don't match up, and her head is slightly *inside* the wall.

Her eyes are open. But the expression is…in panic. Terrified. Frozen. She tries to move. Her arms twitch.

But they don't move right. Like the game is trying to rebuild her… and keeps failing.

I slam my hand over my mouth. *What does this mean?*

The screen **flashes red**.

Once. Twice.

Then black.

Pitch black.

My reflection stares back at me for a second too long.

Then Text. Blunt. Brutal. All caps.

ERROR! CHARACTER REMOVED.

"No. NO.*No no no no no*"
 I mutter, slamming the desk.

"Not again. Not again!"

This wasn't how it was supposed to go. I didn't
even do anything this time. I didn't touch her. I
didn't build her a room. I didn't trap her.
She bloody glitched, this is on the game that this
happened. Not me. Now she's gone.
Erased.
Just like Jeff.
So why does my chest feel tight?
Why do my hands feel numb?
Is it guilt? Or… disappointment?
I shake my head.
No.
This is good. This means Carol will appear back
in the real world. Right?
  If the game is making them disappear in real
life. She'll just... wake up in her bed, maybe a
little groggy. Tell George she had a weird dream.
Go back to work like nothing happened. Say
something passive-aggressive about how dusty
her office was when she got back.
Not dead. Right?
She's not dead.
I didn't kill her.
I didn't do anything this time.
I didn't even touch her.

I didn't build a room. I didn't light a fire. I didn't even remove the goddamn door.

She just glitched.

She wasn't *stable*.

That's the game's fault not mine.

My breath catches in my throat. Unless…Unless she glitched because I made her unstable because of what I forced George to do? And so, the game mimicked that, glitched her out.

The buzzing returns. Quiet now. Lingering. Like static under my skin. The house flickers on the screen, empty.

George is still upstairs. Still wandering in his boxers like he hasn't noticed Carol's gone.

Of course he hasn't. He never noticed her in real life, either.

"It's fine," I whisper. *"Everything's fine."*

I click out of the game.

But the buzzing doesn't stop

Chapter Thirty-One
Memory Dump

George

Brilliant. Back in the void again.

My absolute favourite place. So dark. So quiet. Just me, myself, and the never-ending echo of my own thoughts. I swear this place is somehow worse than the creepy house. At least there, something happens. Here? It's just floating. waiting. existing. Like I am in limbo

This times different though, Carol's not here. Not that I miss her. I didn't exactly win Husband of the Year, but come on, toward the end, I was *done*. Every conversation felt like walking through sludge. It wasn't hate, not exactly. Just… exhaustion. Like we were circling the drain together.

Still, I usually feel her presence here, even in the void. Made me feel less like I was doing this on my own, like I wasn't going insane,

A little nudge of recognition in the dark. But now? Nothing. Maybe we were drugged. Or implanted with something. Something to mess with our memories. Break us down. Make us forget who we were and why we got dragged into this.

Maybe this void is part of it. A punishment. A pause. A test. I don't know.
All I know is I'm alone.
Carol is gone.
Or this is my nightmare, making me finally take responsibility of all the times I have cheated on Carol? It's telling me I need to tell her when I wake up. She's now gone in this dream to remind me of how it will feel without her.

Chapter Thirty - Two
Exe. Pending

Thankfully, it's the weekend. I'm so relieved I don't have to walk into work and hear all the whispering.

"Wonder what happened to Jeff."
"Where's George and Carol?"

I think, it's time to kill in game George. Not because I want to, but because I need to prove to myself that I am not causing these deaths.

It's not fair that Carol glitched, that I had no control over it. She just vanished in the game. Whereas game George hasn't, I don't want to just remove him to see if that just makes him reappear back in real life. That's too easy. Too quick. No... he deserves more than that.
I grab my diary again of scenarios I had wrote down when I was imagining Jeff's torture,
I flip the pages, then find the one I think will fit perfectly for George. A pool. No ladder. A wall around it. Perfect.
He can wait though, first, a food shop. Priorities.
I got to the supermarket real quick today. There

wasn't much traffic for once, and barely anyone was getting on or off the bus. But that didn't stop the buzzing in my skull. I really need to try some sleeping meds or something stronger. I haven't slept properly for days. Even when I do, it's like the game doesn't turn off anymore. I feel it crawling into my thoughts like code running silently in the background of my head.

On the bus, I felt them staring. Not just glancing. Staring. Whispering behind hands and coat collars.

She did it.

It's her fault.

Murderer.

I had to shut my eyes for three whole stops, turn the music up so loud it made my ears ring, just to drown it all out. But even then, their voices pushed through the static. And when one guy muttered

"Carol," I swear my heart stopped. No one reacted but me.

By the time I stepped off, my palms were slick with sweat. I couldn't wait to get off that damn bus.The air outside didn't help. It felt heavy, like stepping out of one simulation and straight into another. I entered the supermarket with a trolley, of course, I picked the dodgy one. The front right wheel squeaked with every turn, that high-pitched screech that makes your teeth tingle and your brain itch. The radio, normally chirpy with happy tunes designed to make you buy more crap was gone. Replaced by a low, broken static, *sssht-sssht-sssht*, like it was trying to pick up a signal from somewhere but was unable to.

I pushed the trolley forward, its wheel shrieking through the aisles, dragging me past shelves I wasn't even looking at. I wasn't shopping. I was moving on autopilot. Tossing items into the trolley without even seeing them.
The static was so loud in my head it drowned everything else out. Words wouldn't come. Thoughts wouldn't land.
Just buzzing. Just noise. I rushed to the checkout like I was being chased. The moment I started placing my items on the conveyor belt, the radio snapped back to life.
Not music. Not a jingle.
News.

"News just in. A body has been found in Suffolk Park. Dismembered. Identity has not been confirmed at this time. However, the police want the public to know they are investigating the matter and will update us when they can. If anyone saw anything

suspicious last night in or around the park, please come forward. Call 999 and ask for Detective Verum…"
I held my breath.

 The urge to abandon my trolley and run was almost unbearable. I looked around, needing to see if anyone else heard it, *really* heard it, that I wasn't alone. The woman behind me leaned into her partner and whispered,

 "Isn't that the second body found now?"

I kept my expression flat. Pretended not to be listening. Pretended not to exist.
But my heart? It was thudding like it wanted out.
Detective Verum. That's who Carol's and Jeff's case was with. Or… *is* with.
 Is it weird he's on this one too? Maybe not.
Maybe he's allowed to take on many cases.
Maybe Suffolk's stretched thin on detectives.
Maybe it's nothing.
But "dismembered"?
I swallow hard.
Carol got splinched in the game. Her body was… everywhere. It won't be her. It can't be her.
Can it?

PART FOUR
REALITY
BLURS

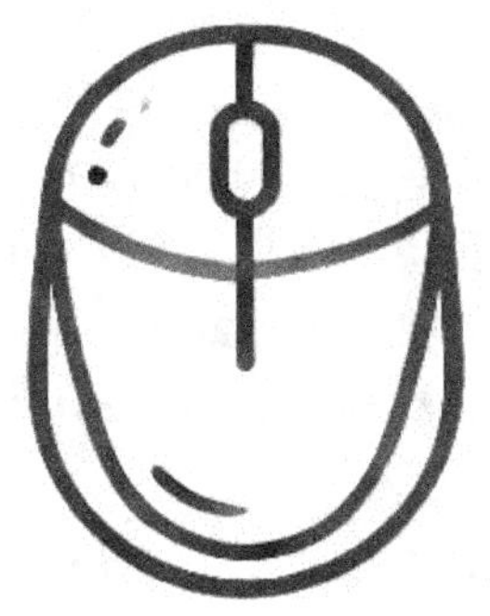

Chapter Thirty-Three
Carved Clean

Detective Verum

I think this case is going to break me.

I was only alerted about the body found at the park because of what was etched on one of the parts thrown around the picnic area.

Play with Me.

Etched. Not scratched. Not scrawled. *Etched.* Clean.

Intentional. Right into one of the upper arms, though it's hard to say which arm for certain until we've put all the pieces back together.

We've got one sick sadist on our hands. No doubt.

But I can't figure out *how* they did it. That's what's eating at me. This body wasn't hacked apart. There are no jagged cuts, no hesitation marks, no saw traces. Normally, when someone dismembers a body, it's messy. Brutal. You can feel the violence in the wounds. This?

This was clean.

Too clean.

The limbs are separated with smooth, calculated precision like they were sliced by a machine.

Surgical, almost. But with none of the markings a blade would leave behind.

I've been trawling through every piece we've found so far, sorting limbs into a main area, logging as I go, while the rest of the team sweeps the perimeter for more. The deeper I go into this scene, the less human it feels.
Then I hear it.

"Detective!"
Hadley. The new lad. I sigh under my breath. Hopefully, he's not crying wolf.

"I think it's the head!" he calls.

I take a deep breath, already bracing for the worst. Hadley looks pale, like he's fighting off the urge to vomit. I walk over to where he is standing.
I clap a hand on his shoulder.

"Go get some water, Hadley. That's an order."

He doesn't hesitate. Just nods and disappears towards one of the police vans.

I step through the overgrown grass and into a
bed of crushed nettles. The sting nips at my legs
through my trousers, but I barely feel it.
Then I see it. Nestled in the greenery, partially
hidden beneath weeds and mud.
A head.
Female.
Short brown bob.
Recognition hits like a punch to the gut.
Oh shit. I crouch, reach out with gloved hands,
and gently lift it by the hair, turning it over.
Of course it is.
Mrs Mendex.
The woman I spoke to just days ago.
Calm. Smiling. Alive.
Now her face is twisted like she was in pain.
Her features look half-formed. Her jaw is
misaligned, her mouth frozen open like she'd
been mid-sentence when something tore her
apart.
   One cheekbone is too high, the other crushed
inward. Her nose is bent at an unnatural angle.
Her eyes, one slightly off-centre which make her
look like she was caught between two
expressions and stuck there.

Deep scratches run down the side of her face. Jagged. Violent. But not deliberately. Not controlled. Like when someone glitches in a game.
I remember my son running into me when one of his characters had glitched like this, he asked me to fix it straight away as it scared him, he was only eight at the time.
I walked over to his computer confidently, so he thought I knew what I was doing,
I looked at the screen, the character was stood in the scarecrow position then when I zoomed in on it's face, it looked like it was slashed. Just like Carols face is now.
 Which obviously can't be what happened. This is real life. Someone just slashed at the face, tried to dismember it. But couldn't finish. I don't speak. There's nothing to say. Nothing that would make sense out loud.
This wasn't rage.
It wasn't a ritual.
It was something else.
Something I don't have a word for yet. Whatever it is, I've got a feeling this isn't the last body I am going to find.

Chapter Thirty-Four
Offline Breakdown

I don't even remember how I checked out at the supermarket.

Couldn't tell you what bus I got on. Hell, I don't even know how I unlocked my front door. All I know is: The second it shut behind me, I dropped. Collapsed onto the floor like my legs couldn't carry me anymore.

I burst into tears.

Hyperventilating.

Rocking like a deranged escaped mental patient.

Fisting my hair in clumps until it ripped from the root.

What the fuck is happening?!

It's just a game.

It's a fucking game.

It's supposed to be a game.

"I'm fine,"

I whisper.

"I'm innocent."

"It's not real."

But that body in the park was real.

That scream echoing in my head, real. The news bulletin real.

I don't want it to be Carol. I need it not to be Carol.
But I have to know.
Even if it kills me, I need to know.
Maybe it's better not to know.
If I don't know, I can pretend it's not linked to me.
Because if it is…
Who would even connect it back?
No one knows about the game.
No one knows I have it.
Even that weird-ass store didn't recognise it.
Except maybe that creep in the chequered shirt.
Maybe *he knew*. Maybe that's why it was on the shelf.
Maybe he wanted rid of it.
Maybe *I* was the next idiot in line.

I drag myself upright using the door handle like it's a lifeline.
My arms feel like jelly. My legs barely hold.
Okay.
Breathe.
In. Out. Count to ten.

I switch on the TV in my bedroom, volume high enough I can hear it while I unpack my shopping in the kitchen.
I open the first bag. Pull out tins. Stack them.
Beans.
Soup.
Tuna.

Normal. Just a normal day.

"News just in…"

My blood turns to ice. I freeze mid-reach, hand still holding a tin of chopped tomatoes. The cupboard door creaks under the weight of my grip. I feel the bile rising up my throat

"The body found in Suffolk Park has now been identified"

I grip the cupboard harder.

"as Carol Mendex, wife of George Mendex, co-founder of The Litterium."

The floor tips sideways. My vision blurs.

"Carol and her husband were reported missing two days ago. George Mendex is still unaccounted for. Police have confirmed this does not appear to be a case of domestic violence. They are urging anyone who may have seen anything suspicious in Suffolk Park to call 999 and ask for Detective Verum."

It *is* her.
Carol.

Carol's dead.

Because of *me*.

No.

No, no, no.

I slide down the cupboard and land hard on my knees.

The tin rolls from my hand and clatters onto the floor.

Then suddenly I am rushing to the sink, throwing up. The realisation of what this means hits me, it makes me physically sick. Everything I have done, I had done to the *real* Carol.

This is not happening.

It can't be.

But the static buzzing in the back of my skull says otherwise.

I know, deep down, that I caused this. Does this make me an abuser?

Chapter Thirty-Five
Free Swim

I pack away my shopping in a daze, barely registering the act. My body's on autopilot, but my brain? Screaming. Running circles. Pushing me toward one thought, I must kill George. Is it to erase evidence? To evaluate the pattern again? I don't know. Jeff could've been a coincidence. Carol… suspicious, but maybe still a freak accident. But if George *dies*, and he ends up like they did?

Then it's real.

Then it's me.

The moment I load the game, there are no butterflies. No excitement. Just that sinking feeling like stepping off a ledge before you realize there's no ground beneath you. That horrible, stomach-churning drop.

The title screen flashes. The red house. The flickering windows. Same as always.

I click **Load Game.**

George is still there alive, in his pants, shovelling food into

his mouth like a Neanderthal. I roll my eyes.

Even in-game, he's vile.

I switch layers to the basement. Pick an empty room. Then I open the build menu and scroll until I find it.

Swimming pool.

I drag the tiles across the room, filling every inch. It's huge. 34 by 34 squares. Only a thin 2-inch ledge around the edge. No climbing out. It even spawns with a ladder.

Not for long.

Once the pool's done, I command George to go in. He huffs, throws his hands in the air like a toddler mid-tantrum. Who does he think he is? I'm the one in control now. Not him. Eventually, he gets there. He jumps in.

I remove the ladder.

Ding.

A pop-up appears.

"Are you sure you want to do that? Without this, your character cannot exit the pool."

Yes / No

I roll my eyes at the game. Doesn't it get it yet? I want to do this. I need to do this.

I click **Yes**.

The screen goes black.

My heart skips.

But then it flashes back to life like nothing

happened. The game doesn't *like* this; I can feel it. The thrum in my head has gotten denser. Like the base of a speaker that's broken.

I switch to full free roam. Let him swim. Let him burn off every calorie he's ever consumed while I go do…anything else. Because I know what's coming.

This time, I'm not going to be able to watch.

Chapter Thirty-Six
Dog Paddle Despair

George

Why the hell am I even in this stupid pool? That pain down my spine hit again, sharp, electric, like something slicing through my nerves. Suddenly I couldn't stop myself. Couldn't think straight. One minute I was in the kitchen, stuffing my face with whatever junk I could find (don't judge me, I was starving), the next I was walking.

I didn't know where I was heading. I didn't *choose* to move. It was like my body belonged to someone else.

Then I was in the pool.

No warning.

No thought.

Just clothes off, jump in, start swimming.

It's only now, now that the buzzing's finally stopped and I've got control back,

 that I realise something's very wrong.

The room has no lights.

I try to swim around the pool, finding the edge to climb out, but the ledge is too narrow. The walls are too high. I reach up, kick, push.

THUD.

My skull hits the side of the pool wall.

"Fuck's sake…"

I swim around again. No ladder. No steps. Just me, floating in a box of water like a goldfish in a tank. It's cold. Getting colder.

What pisses me off more than the temperature, more than the bruises, the darkness, or the waterlogged skin, is that I'm alone.

Again.

I was looking for Carol.

Not because I *miss* her, exactly. I can't even remember what she is to me when I'm here, I have flashbacks of the void thoughts, I know she's meant to be something to me. I just really don't know what we are to each other.

In the dark void, that nothing-space where I float between moments like this, she wasn't there. And I hated that. I hated the silence. Hated the loneliness. Hated not knowing what was happening or where anyone else was. Even Carol. I don't care if she screams at me or rolls her eyes or pretends, I don't exist. At least then I *exist* to someone.

I just need to *find* her. Need to see another face. Even if it's one that looks like it wants to punch me in mine. Because being in this place, alone? It's worse than the dark. At least in the void, I could pretend I was dreaming. Here, I know I'm not, but I also feel this can't be reality. Can it and I think.... this room is where I am going to die.

I left the computer running. Left George on free roam.

Didn't care what he did. Didn't want to know. Sleep, as always, was fitful. My body tried, but my mind wouldn't follow. Every time I closed my eyes, I saw Carol's glitched face. Jeff's scream. I just want to sleep again. Properly. Peacefully. But peace feels like something reserved for the innocent.

A piercing siren jolts me awake. I shoot up, heart thudding in my chest, sweat already gathering at my temples.

That sound, it's not my phone alarm. It's the computer.

The screen is flashing blood red

What the hell? I rush over, nearly tripping on my own feet.

The game's still open. George is still there barely. I can see him, blurry through the static overlay, flailing in the pool like a drunk wasp in a sink. Then I see it.

A message, bold and flashing:

CHARACTER DROWNING: HELP THEM?
YES / NO

My fingers hover over the mouse.
My throat is dry. George. Sleazy, arrogant
George.
 The man who thought it was okay to grope me
at work and then lie about it.
But is that enough to justify… *this*?
I stare at the question.
Help them?
Does clicking no make me a murderer?
What if this really is the final test?
If George dies too, then it confirms everything.
That this game *isn't just a game*. That I'm not
just controlling make believe people.
That I'm killing people.
I shut my eyes. My hand moves on its own.
Click. **NO**
 The screen flashes blood red. The pool fades
from view. Text flickers across the screen.
ERROR: CHARACTER REMOVED
I hold my breath. It's done the same as it did with
Jeff, with Carol.
Gone. I stare at the monitor, frozen. What have I
become?

Chapter Thirty-Eight
Witching hour

Detective Verum

The tone of my phone ringing pierces through my dreams. I open my eyes, roll over to view the Digital Clock on my nightstand.
3AM.

Some say that's witching hour. I say it usually means something bad has happened for someone to be calling me at this time of the morning.

"Verum?"

I grumble into the phone.

"Sorry Detective for calling you so early in the morning, but we've got another body."

"Same markings? Do we know who?"

"Yes, sir. We aren't sure on the body identity though, it's hard to tell."
I rub my hand down my face.

Oh god, what is happening here? Another body. Another Play with Me carved into their skin. Killed in a different way to the last two. Usually, serial killers stick to the same kill method. This one though, nothing. If it's who I think it might be unless there's connections. If it's Mr. Mendex then it's linked to The Litterium.

   Someone in that building has some vendetta. I realised I haven't responded to the person on the phone. The phone's still to my ear and all I can hear is

"Sir, are you coming? Sir, are you there?"
I snap out of my thoughts.

"Yes, where do I need to go?"

"The alley behind Sluggers."

"Okay, I'm on my way."

Chapter Thirty-Nine
Sluggish Alley

Detective Verum

It takes me ten minutes to reach the gentlemen's club. No traffic this time of night, not even the city wants to be awake at 3 a.m.

The alley behind Sluggers reeks of piss, alcohol, and sex. Condom wrappers cling to the gutters like newspapers. Lying right in the middle of it all. Is a body. Sprawled out between discarded bottles and cheap lingerie. Condoms flutter around it, some even stuck to damp patches of skin. At first glance, it looks like a bad joke. A stag night gone sideways. Then I get closer. The body is soaked. Head to toe. Like it has just been pulled from a canal. Water drips steadily from the fingertips, covering the dry ground. Even the hair is drenched, strands plastered to their skull.

There is no canal near here. Not, for miles. If this body was transported, it should have dried at least a little. But this? This body is fresh. Wet. Chlorine hits my nostrils the closer I get. Not algae. Not decay. Not brackish river sludge. Pool water.

I crouch as the medical examiner shifts beside

me.

"What we got?"

I ask, already dreading the answer.

"Male, early sixties. Looks like drowning. I checked his throat, lungs are full of fluid, and his jugular's still holding some. No restraint marks, no signs of struggle. But…"

They pause, tilting the torchlight toward the man's forehead.

"There is a bump. Egg-sized. Dead centre on the front of the skull. No external bleeding, but it is fresh."

I lean in. It's swollen. Red. Probably happened just before he died.

"Could've hit his head trying to escape something," the examiner offers.

"Didn't knock him out though, based on lividity. More like he stunned himself then drowned."

The body is completely naked. The team had checked the alley, and a five-mile radius around

Sluggers for clothes, non were dumped nearby. Not even shoes. It adds to the surrealness of it all. Who the hell strips someone down? I'm still processing that when I notice something else.

Etched, not scratched, right into the side of his neck, in clean, unnervingly straight lines, are three words:

PLAY WITH ME.

Raw red, fresh blood still shining on their skin. Just like the others.

Chapter Forty
Out of Options

It's still the weekend.
Now it's 4 a.m. I feel like I've just snorted guilt and adrenaline straight into my bloodstream. I spent most the night throwing up.

I know I wanted him dead. God, I needed him dead. Watching George flail in that pool, seeing the panic in his stupid smug face as he realised, really realised, there was no way out?
Yeah, it felt good. Too good.
Now I don't know who the hell that makes me.
Because if his body shows up tomorrow.
Then I'm not just a player anymore.
I'm a murderer.
Or at least… an accessory to something? I don't even understand. I shut the computer down. Not just "X" out the game, full shutdown.
 Hold the power button until the screen blinks out like a dying eye.
I even yank the plug from the socket like that'll help.
But the buzzing's still in my head.
Low. Persistent. Like something is loading, just beneath my thoughts.

I don't think I'll play again.

No.

I can't play again.

Not if I turn on the TV tomorrow and see *"George Mendex, co-founder of The Litterium, found dead. Body soaked. Unexplained injuries."* Because that'll be the last straw. That will mean this thing is real. That all of it was real. In all the worst ways. then what?

What happens when the police knock on my door? What happens when Detective Verum puts the dots together?

Will they trace it back to me? The game? Will he ask questions I can't answer without sounding absolutely fucking insane?

A part of me still wants to open the game.

Still wants to build another room.

Choose another name. Just one more time.

But another part, the part that's still sane, still scared, knows if I do, I won't stop. It isn't just having the power to control anymore. It's an addiction.

PART FIVE

CODE

EXECUTED

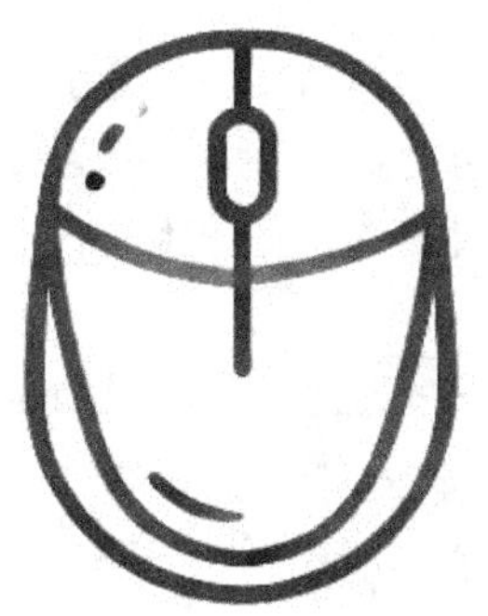

Chapter Forty-One
Accessory Downloaded

I fell asleep with my phone still in my hand, mid-search. I was trying to find anything about other deaths tied to this game, anything on Reddit of other gamers creating people for them to disappear in real life. But there's nothing. Just scattered stories of people dying in odd ways. Electrocution in a dry room. Drowning in bathtubs with no water source. That kind of thing. Creepy, but no solid connections. Nothing about this phrase. Maybe it's copycats. Maybe it's players like me gamers too desperate to hurt people without getting caught.

I didn't want to get out of bed. I still don't. But I need to know. If George has reappeared, dead or alive. I need to see it for myself.

Dragging myself from the mattress, I shuffle across the cold floor toward my TV. I lost the remote months ago, so I have to press the power button like it's 2002. No smart tech here. This TV is ancient. Crusty old buttons and no-HDMI-ports ancient.

If they paid me better, maybe I could've had a bigger place. A separate living room. A massive flat screen. A life that didn't involve people like George grabbing my thigh and Carol telling me to wear less "inviting" clothing.

The anger bubbles up like bile. Fuck Carol. Fuck George.

I gave that company years of my life. in return, I got groped like it was part of my job description.

The TV clicks on. White noise fuzz,
"NEWS JUST IN!"

Chapter Forty-Two
SYSTEM ANNOUNCEMENT

My stomach hollows as I wait for the announcement to finish. It is the same news reporter as last time, the one who seems to report all the deaths. Like they have become the Angel of Death.

"A body has been found near Sluggers, a gentlemen's club. We would like to make clear this is not related to the establishment. The body was discovered around 3AM by a staff member. Here is what the witness has to say—"The screen cuts to a shaky looking man in his twenties, clearly rattled.

"Man, I was just locking up. Went to walk out the alley like normal when I trip over someone's arm. Thought it was another drunk because we get that all the time out there. I was about to kick 'em, y'know, like move! but when I flashed my torch down, I knew something wasn't right. He was shiny. Like, moist shiny. Still. Too still. I shouted. Loud. Nothing. That's when I called 999. I know this kinda thing looks bad on a business, but when a fella's dead in your alley?

You gotta sort it."

The screen jumps again. Detective Verum now takes centre stage. Calm. Collected. Controlled. In his grey suit.

"We reached the scene around 3AM. We estimate the body was placed there between 2:30 and 3. However…"

He pauses.

"We are uncertain how. The condition of the body does not suggest it was moved. It is as if it died exactly where it was found.
Cause of death appears to be drowning, following blunt force trauma to the head. The smell of chlorine was strong, extraordinarily strong. We do have an identification."

That is when I go completely deaf. I slap at the buttons on the side of the TV, fingers numb, adrenaline crashing until the subtitles flicker on. The screen pulses. The light thuds in time with my heartbeat. I can't breathe. Last night, I was woken up at 2:45AM by the computer.

The screen flashing.

The game is humming. He smelled of chlorine. No. It can't be. But then the words crawl across the screen in bold white type:

George Mendex, aged forty-four.

Detective Verum keeps talking. His mouth moves. The words filter through the subtitles. I don't hear the sound anymore. Only the visual. Only the confirmation. George is dead. I already know how.

Because I watched him die.

Chapter Forty-Three
Uninstall failed...

I need to return this game. I rush to get the game out of my computer. I keep pressing the eject button, nothing happens. I will take my whole computer back if I need to.

I do not care that they said no returns. This needs to return to the hell it was found. I grab a knife from my kitchen after searching online how to get the disc tray to open forcefully. I wedge it in the gaps of the tray, angle it into the lip. Sure enough, it clicks open. My PC screen flashes red. I turn to look at it.

"Are you sure you want to do this, Susie?" scrolls across the screen.

I shake my head, look away, turn back. The words are gone. Ugh. This fucking game. My plan is, even if the store is closed today because it's Sunday, I'll post it through the letterbox or slide it under the door. I'm not coming back home with this in my hands.

I get the bus like before. My palms are sweaty, the games in the backpack next to me. I swear it is humming. I hear it in my head. I see my bag

vibrating, pulsing with each throb in my skull. It's okay.
Everything is fine. Breathe.
Look at the seat.
Look at the cars on the road.
I try to ground myself. Stop the thoughts from reoccurring in my head.
 I hate myself. Every time I'm in moments like this; every detail of my life floods back. The way my mom looked at me that one time because I swung my cat by its tail. How it felt when the cat bit me. How it felt to cause that to happen. How an old friend of mine said I was too intense. All the bad stuff floods back. I don't just see it in my mind, I feel it. It's so suffocating.
   I didn't mean to kill Jeff, Carol, and George in real life. I just wanted some control for once in my life . Anger boils inside me. I storm off the bus, ready to give the shop hell for what they've put me through. Only when I get there…
The store's gone.
Gone.
By gone, I mean the buildings not there. It's an empty space. What the actual fuck?!

Chapter Forty-Four
System Override

I gawp at the space where it used to be.
No.
No.
No.
No.
This can't be fucking happening.

I yank my phone out of my pocket and Google the place. I'm in the right location. It even says online that it's still open.

I shout into the empty space, frustration bubbling up and spilling out. My eyes scan the street, desperate for someone, anyone, I can ask what the hell happened.
I spot someone sitting in-between the two buildings where the building used to be. A table in front of them. Maybe they're giving directions? Maybe they know something?
I start running towards them, heart pounding.
Then I see it. A glass orb. Tarot cards. For fuck's sake.

"Give me a break!"
I scream.

The woman behind the table looks up at me, her eyes wide with concern. To be fair, if I saw myself right now, I would be concerned too. I probably look half-feral, eyes wild, sweat sticking to my clothes, to my skin. She studies me carefully. The clouds shift overhead, casting a shadow. Everything gets a little darker. A little colder.

"You are a haunted soul," she says.

"No shit, Sherlock," I snap. *"Tell me something I don't know."*
She doesn't flinch.

"Something's following you. I can feel it. Bad things have happened," she says gently.

"But it wasn't your fault."
Her eyes drop to my bag. My stomach clenches

"There's evil with you," she says, her voice trembling.
"You have to destroy it before it destroys you!"

She starts to shake.
"It's in my head! Make it stop!" she screams, her

voice rising to a pitch that cuts through my bones.

"GO AWAY, SUSIE! GO AWAY! IT HURTS!"

I freeze.
What? My stomach twists.
She didn't say my name.
She couldn't have.
Could she?

"What's in your head?" I whisper, the words dry and shaky on my tongue.

"The game," she spits out, voice no longer her own.

*"Play with me until the lights go out.
Play with me until they can't shout.
Play with me, take control.
Play with me… and take their soul."*

Her voice warps mid-sentence shifting into a robotic echo. Her eyes snap wide open, whites shining in the shadows.

"What have you done?" she hisses.

I don't wait to answer her question. I run. Heart

hammering in my chest like a warning bell. Who *was* that? Is this some twisted publicity stunt by the game store to scare me out of returning it? How the hell did she know the name?

My name? No. No. No. It must be a stunt. It must be

Chapter Forty-Five
System Overheated

Detective Verum

What a night. By the time I got home, it was 6AM. I had to be back at work for 9. I shower quickly, dousing myself in cold water in a half-assed attempt to wake up. If I could shower in bleach, I would, I want to remove the grimy feel of the body off my skin and the stench of the alley.

But I can't.

Soon enough, I'm at my desk. Coffee in hand. Report on my table from the ME with the CCTV camera footage from the alley. This is what I love about this team, efficiency.

I plug the USB into my computer. It whirrs loudly. Damn, my computers never sounded so unhealthy. Might need to ask IT to check it out. I watch the file appear: **CCTV Slugger's Alley**. I open it. I go to an hour before the witness found the body. At first, there's nothing.

Just the alley. Then the moment, the witness steps out into the alley. The camera glitches, goes blurry, then the next frame, there's a body on the floor, the witness stumbling over it. Where did the body come from? Just like the case with Carol. The camera glitches, then *poof,* she's there. Only this time, it's poor George's body. We did get footage of the street where Carol was found too, only because her body was in parts. It was hard to tell where she was dumped, although there was a glitchy frame that gave us a certain point. There's got to be something here. A body can't just *turn up*. I rewind the video, dragging the little dot with my mouse. I pause when it glitches, trying to see if I can catch anything between the broken lines of footage.

I can slightly make out the witness turning to lock the door behind him. The floor, however, is just dark. I do this for another hour. I need a break. I walk over to the coffee machine in the office. The coffee smells rank, but at least it'll keep me awake. I'm running on empty.

I go back to my desk. Lean back in my chair. Crack my fingers. Then stare back at the screen. A dark silhouette of a human figure suddenly moves its way closer and closer to the screen. The closer it gets, the more it glitches, only when it gets in front of the screen, it gets *larger*, and *screams*:

"Play with me! Susie!"

Then, in the blink of an eye, it's gone. Did someone spike the coffee? I only had one sip. I rewind it to see if I can watch it again… but it's gone.

Chapter Forty-Six
Cracking the code...

Detective Verum
"Susie? Susie… Susie."

Why does that name ring such a loud bell in my head?
I grab the interview files we had with some of the employees at the Litterium. I start with Carol's, taken right after we interviewed her about Jeff's death and skim through.

"Jeff was a good guy."
"He's worked here for a few years."
"No, I didn't see him leave."

Then I spot this:
"Susie did report having an incident with him around Christmas.
Found her crying in the toilets. She told me he tried it on with her. She said she didn't want it. But most people know him and Susie have a thing. I didn't believe her."

I knew I recognised her name! But should I really take what someone clearly traumatised said at face value?

It's not like I can remember how I know her, just that I do.

I keep reading. Jeff's file has more interviews.

"Jeff is a funny guy, man."
"We used to play DND together."
"No, I don't spend time with him anymore. Not since he got obsessed with Susie."

There it is again. Her name.

I dig out the other interviews about Carol and land on Linda's.

"Carol was an amazing boss."
"Carol can be a bit strict sometimes."
"But I do know though, she had a vendetta against Susie.
Don't know what happened there but she's always on her case. I'm shocked because Carol wasn't usually like that."

Another incident. Something bad again happening to Susie. Jeff attacked her. So, did George? And Carol didn't believe her?

There's a pattern here.

I think it's time I speak to George's receptionist… Then Susie, face to face.

Chapter Forty-Seven
Corrupt File Detected

I get home, standing in the centre of my room like I've forgotten what home even is. My eyes flick to the computer. I don't sit. I don't touch anything. I just stare at the screen like it's a live grenade, waiting for a twitch.

The game needs to go.

Gone.

Removed.

Erased.

I take a deep breath and power on the computer, hands trembling as if it knows what's coming. I haven't even put the disc back in, but something deep in my gut twists. Something tells me it's already here. Still here.

Sure enough, the *Play with Me* icon is still on the desktop.

Mocking me.

I right-click.

Uninstall.

A progress bar appears. *10%... 20%... 30%...*

I gnaw at my nails, anxiety bubbling up my throat like acid. Every second feels like a year. What if it doesn't work? What if this is all linked back to me eventually?

"You know you and Jeff are close."

 Alexander's voice blares through my skull like a bad recording. Oh, piss off, Alexander. Who else thought that? Who else said it? Did they tell Verum that too?
Suddenly, the screen flashes red. Then black.
And the computer dies.
I stare at it.
Are you kidding me?
I boot it back up. Slow. Painfully slow.
Play with Me is still there.
Of course it is.
I try again.
Right-click. Uninstall.
The process starts… and then crashes. Again.
I try five more times.
Same thing.
Every. Single. Time. I throw myself back from the desk, pace a circle around the room, storm toward my bag, and grab the disc sleeve.
 If I can't remove the files, maybe I can destroy the disc. I slide it out and try to snap it in half. Nothing. Not even a bend. I grab the kitchen scissors, close them against the plastic. They bounce off like the disc is made of titanium.
What the hell is this game made of?!

179

This isn't normal.
This isn't just a game.
It doesn't want to be removed.

Chapter Forty-Eight
Missing files

I've got to go into work tomorrow. I know the detective will be there. There's no way he could have linked all this to me unless people have been running their mouths. I hate how people make assumptions based on one person's point of view. I'd rather people just ask me directly than believe a lie.

I don't know how anyone could think Jeff and I were close. Unless they mistook my sarcastic remarks for flirting. yeah, maybe the way I looked at him before the Christmas incident came off as admiration, only because he was a good friend. His talents amazed me. Nothing more. That all changed after, though. I don't want to go into work, not going will only raise suspicions. I'm going to keep trying to destroy this game before tomorrow arrives.
Might even just throw it in the bin because sitting in landfill is better than someone else playing it, right?

I didn't, I mean, the game didn't kill innocent people I know, but it did kill people. It made people from real life disappear… then die… then pop back up. I wonder what would've happened

if I hadn't killed them… Would they have just stayed missing forever? Is that where all the missing people go?
Someone must have played this game before me. Someone must have created people they know or know of because of human curiosity. There's a whole website dedicated to missing people. Full of faces that vanished without a trace, with no one seeing where they went…
Is this why?
Games like this…

PART SIX

GAME ENDING

Chapter Forty-Nine
Old Nursery Rhymes

Detective Verum

It's Monday. 8:30 a.m. I'm on my way to The Litterium to interview George's receptionist. From what I remember, she's a woman in her late fifties who'd worked with Mr. Mendex for over twenty years. She spoke highly of him during our brief exchange, but I never really dug deeper.

That changes today. I pull into the office car park and step out of my car. My eyes drift to the CCTV cameras. I don't know why. Just... had the urge. It's strange when you think about it, how we're all being watched in some form. Anyone with enough skill can hack into these feeds. People across the country watching strangers go about their day. The thought leaves a sour taste in my mouth. I shake it off, push myself out of that daze, and head toward the elevator

George's office is on the top floor. The elevator dings, and I step inside. Then the music starts. A strange little tune I've never heard before trickles through the speakers, light and high-pitched like

a child's nursery rhyme. But the lyrics are
anything but innocent:

"Play with me until the lights go out.
Play with me until they can't shout.
Play with me, take control.
Play with me… and take their soul."

The melody repeats. A sickly-sweet loop. Like a
horror version of Ring a Ring o' Roses. I freeze
for a second.

"Play with me…"

The same words etched into the victims' bodies.
Someone is messing with me, right? Why is this
song playing here, why was play with me
screamed at me from the CCTV camera
footage?

I reach for my notepad, tug it from my breast
pocket, and jot the lyrics down. I'll investigate it
later. I need to know what it means. The song
loops again as the lift climbs. And again,

Each time it ends, I realise I've been holding
my breath. My shoulders are stiff. My jaw's tight.
The damn song has my skin crawling; goose
bumps raise along both arms. I can't shake the
feeling that this case isn't normal anymore,

there's something more sinister to it.

Chapter Fifty
Repeated Code

Detective Verum

The lift doors ping open. The light just outside flicker on, off, then on again. Not weird at all. The song playing abruptly cuts off mid-lyric.

I shake off the heaviness clinging to me and step out into the lobby. There she is, Meril, the receptionist, looking even gloomier than the last time, I saw her.

"Detective Verum, good morning. Do you have any more news? Have you found the killer?"

She blurts it out before I even get a word in.

"Hi, Meril. We're still looking into who may have done this. As you can guess, with how they died, it's not as straight forward as we'd like. That's why I'm here. I need to interview you again, okay?"

"Again…?" Her voice wavers. "I hope you're not thinking I'm a suspect, Detective Verum. I loved the Mendexes like they were family."

"You're not a suspect" I reply gently.

*"I just need a few more questions answered.
Can we find a room to talk in?"*
She nods slowly.

*"Sure. I guess we can use Mr. Mendex's office…
now that he's not here."*

Tears pool in her eyes. She quickly turns her face away, so I won't see. We walk together down the hall, Meril leading the way and she opens the office door, stepping inside to flick on all the lights. It's like any other CEO's office: oversized desk, polished wood, a wall of shelves, framed photos of smiling family scattered around. I forgot they had a daughter until her face stares back at me from behind the desk in one of the frames. Telling her about her parents was hard. I had to call her. She was abroad, on holiday with her boyfriend.
When I told her, her scream pierced straight through me. Stephen, her boyfriend had to take the phone from her. She couldn't speak. She was in agony. No child expects to be told both of their parents aren't coming home.

Chapter Fifty-One
Questions to code Answered.

Detective Verum

I cough, pulling myself out of the memory.

"Meril, take a seat,"
I say. She does.

"So, the last time we spoke, I didn't really ask you much about how the Mendex's were. We only discussed what you thought of them."

"Correct," she replies.

"I've read through some interviews with other colleagues of yours. One name keeps coming up. Could you tell me the story of Carol and Susie?"

She takes a sharp breath, like she's shocked it's been brought up.

"Okay, well… Erm, I wasn't there for all of it. I only saw the end. George had asked me to call Susie up to his office, so I did. She went in, they spoke. Then I went to the toilet. When I came back, Carol was in the office too. She was

shouting at Susie. Next thing I know, Susie's running out of the office in tears."

"Hmm. Did you ask what happened?"

"See, I didn't have to, because Carol's a close friend of mine. The moment she came out the office, she told me. She said she walked in on George and Susie, but they weren't talking. She saw Susie trying it on with George. She said Susie was standing in front of him, face close, like she was about to kiss him."

"Did you believe what Carol said?"

"Okay… so here's the thing and please, don't tell anyone. I don't think Carol even knew. But George. He's had female employees up to his office a lot. When I've gone in to give him his coffee, I've seen him being very handsy with them. I never said anything. I didn't want to lose my job. I did try to talk to him about it once, but he got… scarily angry. So, after that, I just pretended I didn't see it anymore. I felt bad for Susie, but I could never tell her I knew the truth. Because if I did, it'd get back to Carol."

She says it all so fast, like she's scared if she pauses, she'll lose her nerve. One long breath, and it's out.

So, once again, Susie was sexually assaulted. The two men who did it? Missing, now confirmed dead. The person who knew about both incidents but didn't believe her? Also missing, and now also dead.
Is this all just a coincidence?
Or is our killer… Susie?

"Meril, I need you to call Susie here."

Chapter Fifty-Two
Run CMD

I'm now at my desk, the strongest coffee beside me because sleep didn't happen. When it finally did, it was nothing but screams. Screams of everyone I've killed in the game.
I boot up my computer.
Suddenly, my phone rings.

It's Meril, she was George's receptionist, I guess she isn't anymore. How are we all still working without a manager or a CEO?

"Hi Meril, you, okay?" I answer, trying to sound casual.

"Hi Susie. I'm fine," she replies, but her tone is off. Way off.

"Detective Verum's here…" she continues. *"He wants to interview you. Can you come up here, please?"*

What? Why? Why the hell does he want to interview me? I haven't even been on his radar. So why now? How?

Like hell I will. I grab my stuff and head straight for the exit. He's onto me. I know he is. I can't go to jail. I can't be held responsible for these murders. If I try to explain how it all happened, they'll lock me in a mental health ward before I even finish the sentence.
Imagine saying this out loud:
A game I bought made real people disappear. When I killed them in the game, they reappeared in the real world, exactly how they died in-game.
    No one would believe me. They'd laugh. They'd call me insane. I pack all my stuff, run out the fire exit, run down the stairs like someone chasing me, because mentally it feels like the Detective is chasing me.

Chapter Fifty-Three
Code Missing

Detective Verum

I sit here waiting, each second dragging louder than the last. The ticking clock in Mendex's office might as well be a goddamn drumline.
Five minutes pass. Ten. Fifteen. That's enough.
I push back from the desk and head out into reception. Meril's typing away like she's still got a boss to impress. Maybe she just doesn't know how to stop working.

"Meril,"
I say, approaching her desk,

"Did you call Susie like I asked?"

You never know, she might've forgotten the second she left the room.
She blinks up at me, a little haughty.

"Of course I did, Detective. She said she'd be right up. Do you want me to call her again?"

I nod. My gut's twisting. Not Meril's fault, but everything in me is saying Susie was never planning to show up.
Meril picks up the phone and dials. The line rings once, twice.
Then clicks as someone answers.

"Oh, Linda?"
Meril says, surprised.

"Hi, it's Meril. Is Susie around?"
Pause.
Her face falls a little. She looks at me, then cups the receiver slightly.

"It's Linda."
I motion for her to put it on speaker. She does.
Linda's voice crackles through.

"Susie? No, she's not here."
"Do you know where she went?"
I ask, stepping closer to the desk

"She was supposed to come see me."

"She… left," Linda replies, hesitant

"Got a phone call at her desk. No idea who it was. The moment she hung up, she packed up her stuff. Like frantically. Just grabbed her things and ran. Didn't even say goodbye. I thought it was some kind of emergency."

"Emergency?"

I echo, more to myself.

"Yeah. She looked… scared," Linda adds. *"Did something happen?"*

I don't answer. I'm already turning toward the door. She's gone. I've got to find her. Before I leave, I shout over to Meril

"Email me Susie's Address and phone number"

"Of course" Meril responds, I hear her tapping away as I rush out the door.

Chapter Fifty-Four
Digital Ghosts

God, I can't breathe. It feels like the whole world is closing in on me, the only thing that went in my favour is the bus. It pulled up just as I got to the stop. No waiting. No thinking.
Now I'm on it. Cramped seat. Shaking legs.
I can't sit still.
I'm fidgeting so bad the guy next to me keeps side-eyeing like I'm about to explode. I feel like I am. I'm seconds away from bursting into a full-on metal breakdown. One that would definitely cause someone to call 111 to check my welfare. My hands won't stop shaking.

I keep my head down, I swear, every single person on this bus is watching me. I feel it. Like they know. Like they've already seen my face in a news article:

"If you see her, call the police immediately."

Has there been a report already? A photo of me, grainy CCTV footage, my name in bold font? want to check. I also don't want to check. I can't breathe. I can't think. My chest is caving in and the world's spinning.

Why did I do it?

I didn't have to kill them. I could've played the game differently. I could've… I don't know. Built houses. Made them dance. Watched them fall in love. I didn't have to. But I did.

Not even all of them. I didn't kill Carol. The game killed her. Glitched her out of existence. I watched it happen, but I didn't click anything. I didn't choose that. That wasn't me.

Still. I ran. I shouldn't have run.

I couldn't sit there. I couldn't let Verum look me in the eye and see the truth. I couldn't let him ask about the game, about the murders, about how I bought something from a store that no longer exists.

How do you explain something like that?

You can't.

You get locked up. In a prison or a psych ward, it doesn't matter. It doesn't matter if you can prove it. They wouldn't let you show them, the truth. How would I even show them? Create someone in front of him, watch them disappear. Then what? I don't know how to make them reappear into the real world without killing them.

I press my forehead to the bus window. The glass is cool, grounding. My thoughts won't stop racing and then… an idea. I've searched everything about what the game does but not where it came from. Not once. I never tried to find the people behind it.

 Someone out there must have made this game. Someone must know what it is. I unlock my phone with shaking fingers, type:

"Play with Me game origin."
Something loads.

Top result:
 "Play with Me: The Game That Shouldn't Exist"
Right beneath it, the tagline:

"A cursed digital experience—rumour or reality?"

I don't hesitate.
I tap the link.
The screen flashes.

SYSTEM ERROR 404. PAGE NOT FOUND.

You've got to be kidding me.

"OF FUCKING COURSE!"

Heads on the bus turn. I don't care.

Why did I expect anything different?

Of *course,* the game wouldn't let me find out how it was made. Of course, it would lead me right to the edge of something real and then slam the door in my face.

This game isn't just haunted.

It's alive.

It's aware.

It doesn't want me asking questions.

It's in control.

Chapter Fifty-Five
The Suspect

Detective Verum

I take the stairs two at a time, running down floor after floor like the buildings on fire. There's no way I'm getting in that lift again. I can't stomach another round of that sick little tune playing over the speakers while I stand there, trapped.

By the time I hit the bottom floor and burst into the car park, I'm gasping. Bent over, hands on knees, dragging in lungsful of air like I just sprinted a marathon.

She ran. Why did she run, if she is innocent?

Susie's involved; she must be. She's at the centre of this, the one link between every missing person and everybody that's turned up dead. But how? If it's the Susie I remember, she's petite. Slight. Barely tall enough to pass a height restriction at a theme park. There's no way she could lift a body, let alone dismember one.

Unless it was all done in a rage. Adrenaline can turn a person into something else. Something feral. Women with PMDD go in blind rage, not realising what they've done until it's over with.

There's a case where a woman killed her husband, she blamed PMDD.
The psychologist deemed it plausible. So, she didn't get prosecuted for murder, not even manslaughter.
Did Jeff try to hurt her again?
Did George make a move?
Did Carol call her a liar one too many times?
What pushed Susie over the edge?
How the hell didn't I see this before?
We had Jeff's phone. There was a message from him to Susie. I remember skimming it, something flirty, harmless. We brushed it off. But did we ever look at the rest? Did we even check the full message history? Did she even reply to him? Goddamn it.

How many times have we mistaken the dead for the victim, when they were really the predator? It doesn't diminish the fact they were murdered; it just allows us to see the cause.
I climb into my car, slam the door shut, and tap Susie's address into the satnav. **Destination: 30 minutes away.** I turn the key in the ignition, the engine roaring to life.
I'm coming, Susie.
I want the truth.

Chapter Fifty-Six
The Countdown

The second the bus hisses to a stop, I'm up. Practically throwing myself down the steps, nearly trip over some guy's foot. I don't look back. I'm too busy running.

My legs are jelly. Every muscle burns. I can barely hold my phone; I'm shaking that badly. My clothes are soaked in sweat. I can *smell* myself and not in the "been to the gym" way. This is panic. Raw, sour, survival-level panic.

I reach my apartment building, open the reception door. A blazing out of order sign is on the lift. No, not today, why now? It's like the universe wants me to get caught. I take a deep breath, stopping myself from screaming again. I rush over to the door that leads to the stairs. I need to not waste time. I need to not think about how long it will take me to get to my apartment.

"Please, if there is a god, allow me to do this" I whisper as my trainer slams onto the first step.

I am a sweaty mess when I finally get to my door, my feet are numb, my legs ache, but I did it. My hand goes to my jacket to find my key, only It's not there, I check the other pocket not there.

I feel hot tears roll down my face in frustration. I feel my chest tighten. Calm down Susie, it's got to be here somewhere, I empty my bag on the floor. Rifle through everything, it's not there.

My stomach starts flipping. I close my eyes, trying to picture where I had placed my key, I was in a rush, flashes of me grabbing everything off my desk go through my head. Then I see it, my hand reaching out for my keys, placing them in my jeans pocket. I sigh, relief floods over me, I tap my front jean pocket, I hear the jingle. I rip them out my jeans. They tumble out of my hands. The crash of them hitting the floor echoes through the corridor.

"Come on, come on, come *on*"

I scoop it up, jab it into the lock, twist.
I'm inside. Slam the door. Lock it. Bolt it. Chain it.
Then I just stand there, in the middle of the front room, gasping. I feel like I've run a marathon while being hunted. I pace Back and forth.
Back and forth.

I flick the TV on. The news hums to life, boring updates, political crap, weather, sports. Nothing about a suspect on the run. No

"Breaking story" about *"Susie Carmichael being wanted for questioning."* No CCTV images. No dramatic headlines.
But that doesn't mean he isn't coming.
It just means he hasn't announced it yet. My phone buzzes.
I snatch it from the sofa and look.

A text from, Linda.

"Detective Verum called your phone. He's looking for you. Where are you? Meril had to give him your address. What's going on?"

I freeze.
Then scream.

"NO! NO! FUCKTY FUCK FUCK!"
I throw the phone across the room. It bounces off the wall, lands somewhere behind the table.
He knows.
He knows where I live.
That means he could be here in minutes. Okay, wait. Think.

I had at least a fifteen-minute head start, maybe more. If he stayed to ask questions… if he had to get in the lift, get to his car, tap in directions… That gives me maybe forty-five minutes, tops. Forty-five minutes until he's outside that door. Unless he speeds.
I don't know what to do. I feel like I'm going to be sick. My whole body's trembling. I wipe sweat off my forehead with my sleeve and stare at the desk. At the computer. At the game.
The game that started everything. And then… the thought creeps in. What if…
What if I create myself in the game? Would It..
No.
Would it actually… put me *in*?
No, that's insane.
It wouldn't. It *couldn't*….Right?
I stare at the monitor.
The screen glows, soft and cold.
The words **Play with Me** flash on the screen again.
Once.
Twice.
Then gone.
Like it's teasing me. Like it *knows* what I am planning.
It shouldn't be there.

I know that. I haven't touched the game since George died. Never rebooted. It shouldn't be running.

My stomach turns. I feel like I'm being dared. Mocked.

Come on, Susie. Just one more game.

Maybe I should, one last time.

I grab my bag, unzip the front pocket with trembling hands, and pull out the disc. It's ice cold in my fingers like it's been sitting in a freezer, not in my nice warm bag.

I walk to the computer.

My finger hovers over the eject button for a second too long. I don't want to press it.

But I do. **Click.**

The disc tray groans open slowly, like it's waking up from a long sleep. Dust shifts in the fan vents. The tray closes, The screen pulses. **Play With Me** appears again, bolder this time. Waiting.

Chapter Fifty-Seven
Obstruction Ahead

Detective Verum

The GPS says twenty minutes. I've been on the road for thirty. I grip the wheel tighter, watching the traffic ahead crawl like a funeral procession. Every red light, every hesitant driver, every damn cyclist, it's all in the way.
I've tried calling Susie six times.
Voicemail. Every time.
She's not answering because she doesn't want to.
Or because she's doing something she doesn't want me to stop.
I slam my palm against the steering wheel.

"Move!"
No one moves.
I yank the handbrake and swerve the car up onto the pavement.
Pedestrians scatter. A woman screams. I lean out the window, shouting,

"Police! Get out the way!"

 I'm not waiting in traffic while a potential killer
tries to run away.
Not today.

Chapter Fifty-Eight
Final Upload

The game finishes loading. The screen pulses like a heartbeat. **Create a Character** flashes in bold across the menu. I don't click it. Not yet.

My fingers twitch as I reach for my bag. I dig out my camera, flip it on, and snap a photo of myself, right now. Wild hair. Eyes ringed with exhaustion. Face slick with panic sweat.
This is who I am. Who I Really am.
I hold the camera, staring down at the image.
I glance at the computer. The fan is humming louder now, like it knows. Like it's urging me forward.
But I hesitate.
If I go into the game… he can't find me.
He'll think I ran. That I skipped town, vanished into thin air. He won't imagine I'm still here in the apartment, technically.
And even if he does? Even if he opens the game and sees *me*?
He'll never believe it's really me.

Who would? People create themselves in games all the time. He won't know that only in this game, it takes the actual person into them game.... Right?

  Still, the idea circles my mind like a vulture. When a character dies in the game, their file disappears.
No trace. No recovery. Wiped clean. At least, I think that's what happens. If he takes the game into evidence, there will be no proof of me loading Jeff, Carol or George in the game. I hope.

PART SEVEN

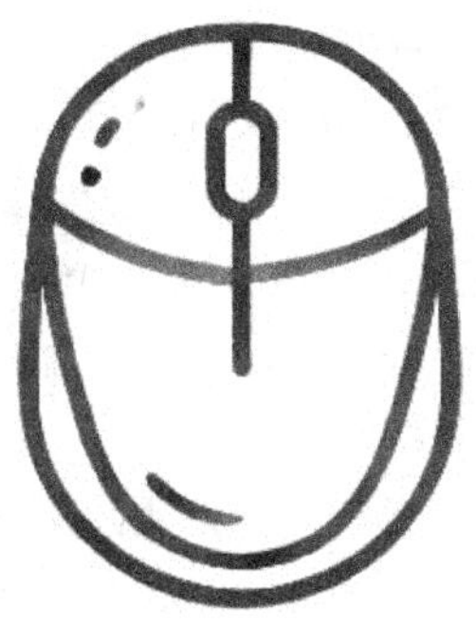

The Final Upload

Chapter Fifty-Nine
No Elevation

Detective Verum

I park like a maniac outside the block. No time to find a spot. I jump out, badge flashing as I shove past the buzz-in door.

Of course she lives in a block of flats. Of course, Because the universe clearly hates me, I get inside only to find the lift is broken, out of service, taped up like a crime scene.

"Fantastic,"
I mutter, already moving.

She lives on the top floor.
This is going to absolutely kill me.
I take the stairs two at a time, lungs already burning, boots thudding against concrete. My mind races faster than my feet.
Calling for back up as I go

"Suspect on the run, I repeat Suspect on the run, need back up"
I tell them her address.

Chapter Sixty
Now or Never

   The photo finishes transferring to my computer. The screen pings. Image ready.
I freeze.
I think I hear something outside.
Footsteps? A voice? My windows are open. I left them that way to stop myself overheating but now every sound from the street below feels like it's *inside* my apartment. Crawling up my spine.
Is he here? Already?
I rush to the window, peek out.
Nothing.
But the panic's already in motion. It floods my chest like ice, spreads through my limbs like fire. My throat tightens. My hands won't stop shaking.
It's now or never, Susie.

Chapter Sixty-One
Devil at the Door

Detective Verum

I finally reach the top floor, breath heaving, heart pounding like a war drum. The corridor is long and dimly lit. I scan the doors.

662… 664… 666.

Of course.

The devil's number. How fucking poetic. I walk straight up to the door and knock. Hard.

"Susie? It's Detective Verum. I need to speak with you."

No answer.

Chapter Sixty-Two
Too Late to Turn Back

Oh fuck.

He's found me.

The knock echoes through the flat like a shotgun blast. I grab the mouse, slam the image into the game folder. It flickers for a second like the game is absorbing it.

I click **Create Character**.

My face appears.

I click **Upload**.

Chapter Sixty-Three
Empty Room

Detective Verum

I knock again. Louder.

Still nothing. I press my ear to the door. A sound. Whirring. Like a fan. No, it's deeper than a fan, a duller hum.

Something's happening in there. I take a step back. Then I kick the door in. It bursts open with a crack. I storm inside.

No one, is there. The flat is empty. Absolutely empty. But it's not clean. Clothes. Bags. Open drawers. A toppled chair. Everything's scattered like she was panic packing. Did she know I was coming? Did Meril tip her off or Linda? I know, she was just here. Where has she gone? I cross the room in two strides and stop in front of the computer.

It's on. There's a game running.

I stare at the screen.

A house, built in-game. Cartoonish, almost playful, Then I see her. A character. Standing in the middle of the house. Waving.

Waving *up at the screen*. She looks just like Susie.

Exactly like Susie. The same wild eyes. Same messy hair. Same expression I saw in the photo attached to her HR file.
The character blinks.
Still waving.

"What the hell is this game?" I whisper.

Acknowledgements

This book has been a journey, one that's been just as twisted, unpredictable, and haunting as the story itself.

To my ARC readers: You were the first brave souls to dive into this cursed world. Your excitement, reactions, and goose bumps made me believe in this story all over again. Thank you for messaging me, for staying up late thinking about Susie, and for wanting more even when it got dark. You don't know how much that means to me.

To Zoe: Thank you for listening to me ramble when this idea was just a strange whisper in my head. You heard the chaos before it became real, and your support helped bring this twisted thing to life. You were there before Susie had a voice, before Jeff had a face, before I even knew how deep the game would go.

And to the voices in my head (aka Susie, Jeff, Carol, George, and Verum): You wouldn't shut up, and honestly, I'm grateful. You made this book what it is dark, messy, human.

If you got this far. Go on turn the page and see what's next!

— Fiona Myers

Sneak Peek of Catch Me

Susie's gone; I look around her room trying to find out some hint of where she might have absconded to. The team arrived a few minutes ago, they're going through her belongings. I feel tense, irritable, my jaw aches from grinding my teeth together, waiting for one of them to find something.

"Detective"

 I feel myself physically jump. No-one has spoken for hours as they comb through the apartment. Everyone in here, has been helping on the case since day one. They want to solve these homicides as much as I do.

"Yeah, have you found something?"
 I ask the officer

He has a notepad in their hand. Oh, please say Susie wrote down something, to make sense of all that's happened. The past few weeks have been some sort of feverish dream. People disappearing with no reason or trace. Then reappearing in the oddest of places, with words etches on them that no-one understands. Except maybe Susie.

   I walk over to them with my hand outstretched. They pass me the note pad. I turn it over in my hands, it has a black cover with the words Diary Tipp-Exed on the front.

I flip through the pages, skim reading, the first twenty odd pages is Susie moaning about working at the Litterium, but then the words "Play with me, The Game" in capital letters appear. I stop flicking. The page flops open. Susie had written a bunch of words down, but clear as day there is Jeff's, Carols and George's name.

"Okay everyone, I want this diary and the game out of the computer bagged and put into evidence."